The Sheik's Captive

By

Honey Jans

Honey Jans

This is a work of fiction. Names, characters, places, and incidents are products of the author's imagination or are used fictitiously and are not to be construed as real. Any resemblance to actual events, locales, organizations, or persons, living or dead, is entirely coincidental.

The Sheik's Captive by Honey Jans

Red Rose Publishing

Copyright© 2007 Honey Jans
ISBN: 978-1-60435-917-6
Cover Artist: Nikita Gordyn
Editor: Lea Schizas

Red Rose™ Publishing
www.redrosepublishing.com
Forestport, NY 13338

Thank you for purchasing a book from Red Rose™ Publishing where publishing comes with a touch of Class!

Chapter One

"Honor Blackwell, you are in way over your head," I muttered to myself as I broke into jewel thief Ali Baba's tumbledown Mediterranean villa. Well not exactly broke in since the door was unlocked. It was a technicality, one I'd cling to since I hated the thought of breaking the law.

I was an artist not a PI but when the opportunity to get away from my obnoxious boss's lecherous advances and make a fat fee that would insure my future came up, I'd jumped at it. This boon would enable me to quit my part time jobs and concentrate on getting my paintings ready for my spring showing.

I had my dad's homemade mace in my tote bag, not to mention handcuffs, and the American Embassy and my client's number on speed dial. I was ready. All I had to do was grab the necklace and get back on the ferry to the mainland.

As promised, the villa was deserted, the thief supposedly out for his afternoon swim. This simple dwelling told me that while the gigolo with the cutesy nickname might have succeeded in relieving my client of her necklace he was far from successful. He was probably young and cocky with a ready smile and a smooth line. Not my type at all.

Actually, the shack reminded me of the tiny lakeside cottage I'd grown up in while my father had his scrapes with the law.

I caught sight of my reflection in the mirror and bit back a groan. I looked like I'd just been through an ordeal, traversing a goat path to this guy's hide out. My feet ached in the little pink sandals I wore. The sundress I'd worn to blend in with the tourists clung to my too full curves, and I was glowing, probably sunburned I decided firmly. I needn't have bothered trying to blend in.

Apparently not many visitors came to this remote island on the Mediterranean. I rejected the thought that I was getting off on this, even though my heart was racing, my senses alive with excitement. My honey blond hair had escaped the chignon I'd put it into, to curl around my shoulders.

My goals had been clear since the first time I'd picked up a paintbrush. I'd get ahead, not like the gigolo did by using my body. Not that anyone was asking, except Hal my obnoxious boss who still wanted to marry me, even though I was a dud in bed. Who needed the prig, at least my vibrator got me off, kind of. Big red was still in my suitcase back in my Athens's hotel.

My fascinated gaze swept the simple room, the major feature being the king sized bed. Ali Baba probably used every inch of it for his sex-capades. His leather shaving kit sat on a dresser as promised. According to my client, it was where he hid his loot. Knowing I needed to hurry, I rushed toward it. Tearing open the leather bag, my eyes widened when I noticed the box of condoms, king sized. The gigolo obviously had an inflated opinion of himself.

As promised at the bags bottom was a secret compartment. I felt inside, my fingers closing with triumph around cool stones. It was here. My client wasn't nuts after all. I pulled out the emerald necklace and let out a little gasp at its beauty. Whoever had cut and set the stones was a gifted artist. My heart raced as I examined the beautiful necklace, the stones glowing with an inner green fire that took my breath away. On my salary, I'd never be able to afford such a masterpiece, but I could still admire it.

The thump of a door closing made my heart stop as I clutched the stolen goods in a death grip. He was back, early. My accursed client hadn't been right about his timetable after all. Shit. My spine stiffened as I tried to surreptitiously tuck the necklace into my straw tote bag, and then I slowly turned around. I didn't want him to think I was making a false move, give him an excuse to shoot me.

Who knew what kind of desperado I'd be dealing with? My eyes widened when I caught sight of the swarthy hunk's naked splendor. He was unarmed if you discounted his impressive cock that swelled as he looked back at me. He wasn't at all what I'd expected him to be, older, with a confident air about him that made me wonder if he was innocent. I gazed into his chocolate brown eyes seeing suspicion that was quickly replaced by a lazy sexual fire. Whoa! My mind called out run but I couldn't seem to move.

Instead, I straight out ogled him back. Droplets of seawater sparkled in his raven dark hair. Aggressively male, and handsome as sin, he looked like he didn't need a weapon to take me down. Hell, I was in deep trouble.

As soon as this was over, I was going home to Wisconsin and investing in a whole brace of vibrators. My gaze locked with his dark eyes and my sex quivered. I gulped as his amused gaze flicked from me to the sandy footprints I'd tracked all over his tile floor. Heart pounding a mile a minute, I froze.

My hungry gaze tracked a glistening drop of seawater down his muscled chest and washboard abs, to circle around his huge cock. I instantly took back that inflated ego crack. He was huge; not that I'd had that many men strip for me.

His manhood hung halfway down his muscled thigh. He noted the direction of my stare; his sultry mouth kicking up into a bad boy grin that set my hormones haywire.

My body tingled coming alive even though I told myself to cool it. Flames raced through me telling me that wasn't going to happen anytime soon.

"Well, well, what do we have here?" he said, stepping toward me. "I told my brother not to send me a present."

I almost fainted as his honey dark tones washed over me, making my sex pulse, my nipples tingle. He sounded even better than he looked, and he thought I was his love gift. I'd never been mistaken for a seductress before, it was kind of exciting.

If only he knew how unresponsive I was in bed. I immediately suppressed that depressing thought. How could I deny that I was there to make love to him without admitting that I was here to steal the necklace back? Why else would I be in his room? He was already suspicious of me, I could tell. He could have me thrown in jail, or worse. I shuddered to think of spending time in a foreign jail.

Apprehension made my knees quiver, even as it crazily increased my inappropriate sexual response. By now, a sheen of moisture coated my thighs as my clit stiffened. I didn't even get this response with my vibrator. The hunk gave off some wicked pheromones to affect me this way.

I pulled my jangled senses together long enough to give him what I hoped was a sultry smile. "Happy birthday...."

"Alexander, Sheik Alexander Kahn."

I tried not to roll my eyes at the alias and played along. Let him have his fantasies. My warped brain was coming up with a few of my own. "As in 'being carried off into the burning sands by my sheik'?"

His eyes twinkled. "It can be arranged."

Trembling as he closed in on me, I couldn't have run if I'd wanted to. I didn't want to. My legs weren't working, and some crazy part of me wanted to stay; soak in a little more of his sexy essence. Madness, but I couldn't deny it. When his hot glance lingered on my breasts, my nipples tightened as if by his command, and I bit my lip embarrassed.

He smiled grasping my shoulders, holding me fast.

My bare arms burned at the contact and I sucked in a shocked breath as he bent to kiss me. "What are you doing?"

"Trying a sample of your wares, Miss..."

"Honor," I said with a moan as his firm lips slanted over mine. He tasted like coffee and hot man mixed with a salty tang from the sea. Like the sex-starved spinster that I was, I dove in.

I kissed him back, my tongue parrying with his, my body aflame as he pulled me closer. I didn't need much coaxing to press against him, feeling his rippling muscles, his hot flesh, the demanding thrust of his cock.

My breasts pillowed against his hot chest making my nipples throb while his rousing manhood pressed against my quivering pussy. I melted, arching against him, helplessly turned on and not knowing how to handle it, or him.

My hands came up to brace myself against his chest, and my fingers dug in kneading his pecs making him growl. A shiver went down my spine at his hot response.

When I felt him slide the bag from my shoulder and heard it hit the floor I was too caught up in his sensual spell to react. The sibilant rasp of my zipper being lowered broke the spell. I pressed my hands flat against his chest pulling back. "What are you doing?"

"Unwrapping my present, Honor."

Hell, why had I given him my real name? Hearing the sexy way he said it made me cream. The heated look in his eyes as he watched me said he read my every emotion. It almost made me bolt, but I didn't want to. Running wasn't an option anymore. His challenging gaze almost dared me to object.

I pressed against him instead, loving the feel of this hunk's body. Not love I amended. I was going to be sophisticated about this and take a sample from him, as well. Still, I let out a gasp when my dress fell, pooling at my feet. Blushing as his sultry gaze swept over me in my pink lace bra and panties, I suddenly felt embarrassed, shy. My curves were too plump, and nobody had ever accused me of being a beauty. When I put my arm up to cover my breasts, he took my hand stopping me.

"Do not try to hide your beautiful jewels from me."

My pussy rippled at his words, then he urged my hand down to his cock, and I wrapped my fingers around his steely heat entranced. Good grief, I could hardly hold him. I tested the silky strength of his hard on making him jerk, thrilled when he lengthened even more in my grasp. My body quickened as I jacked him off.

Shit, this was madness I thought, my thumb sliding over the drop of cum on his slit, making him swear in Arabic. His reaction thrilled me. I never affected men this way.

When he unhooked my bra, and pulled down my panties I was too turned on to do more than blush. Then he touched me, his hand slipping between my quivering thighs, and I closed my eyes with a moan of pure pleasure. He was so much better than...big red.

I throbbed in his hands, his fingers filling my pulsing sheath, his thumb homing in on my sensitive clit. I let out a gasp as he played with me and then he bent to suck one of my stiff nipples into his hot mouth and I screamed. The twin sensations sent me sailing and I put myself fully into his control.

He propped my foot on a hassock to open me shamelessly and I just whimpered in approval as his fingers went deeper into my sex. His masterful touch completely seduced me. He pressed my clit hard, closed his teeth over my nipple and I came, crying out as spasms wracked me. "Oh my god," I cried out, falling against him. It was nothing like the weak response I got from my vibrator.

"I've got you, love," he said scooping me up into his arms.

I clung to him, my racing pulse slowing as I came back to earth. I felt movement and opened my eyes in time to see him carry me into the bathroom. What the hell was he up to? Now that my head wasn't filled with lust, I knew it was crazy to stay...I had to leave, catch the ferry. "Stop...what are you doing?"

"Washing the salt off me," he said, turning on the shower.

I tried to wiggle out of his arms, but his grasp tightened as he gave me a resolute stare. I suddenly knew he meant to keep me. I should scream, although who would hear me but a goat. I should at least try to hit him in the nads and run. Instead, I let out a pleasured groan when he stepped us both under the pulsing spray. I suddenly felt boneless as I snuggled in his strong arms. The damned shower felt good, and my sheik felt even better. I was so getting fired for this, but I didn't care.

His dark gaze on mine made my body quicken again, my sex pulse anew. What was he thinking? My eyes shut when he muttered what sounded like a curse and bent to kiss me. At least I wasn't the only one feeling conflicted. The kiss was hard and demanding, not playful like before and I found myself kissing him back just as hungrily.

I had to memorize him because I knew I'd never meet another man like him. My arms tightened around his neck, my tongue flicked over his lower lip and he gentled the kiss, seeming to savor me. Still kissing me, he let me go to slide down his slick body.

The erotic sensation blew my mind. I stood on trembling legs, leaning into his hard strength absorbing him. There was no way I could go back and get engaged to Hal after this. The thought made me smile. At least this interlude had made up my mind for me.

When he broke the kiss and set me back on my heels I looked at him through a steamy orgasmic cloud. He was absolutely perfect. I wanted him again, and I'd have him before I caught the ferry out of here. My heart pained at the thought of leaving but I pushed it from my mind. I had a man to seduce. He picked up a sea sponge and sandalwood body wash and thrust them at me with a sultry smile.

"Wash me concubine."

"What did you call me?" I took them from him seeing his lips twitch with amusement.

"Concubine...a sort of wife in training."

I throbbed at his words. I wasn't ever going to marry, it wasn't in the cards.

Still, as his hot glance swept over me, lingering on my breasts, I could hardly concentrate on my objections. The scent of my sexual arousal hung heavy in the air and I knew he liked it when his nostrils flared. His wicked cock bobbed before me, throbbing and unsatisfied. He'd given me pleasure without taking any for himself; it wasn't the act of a criminal, maybe he could be redeemed.

"Not a wife, please," I teased lathering his chest with the soapy sponge.

"You're not interested in marriage," he said, his brow quirking.

He didn't believe me. I gazed at his doubtful expression, reminding me of his look when he first found me standing in his bedroom. Why would a man like him be interested in my views on marriage?

I'd think he'd probably run the other direction if a woman tried to put a ring on his finger. "Marriage is an outdated custom. Believe it or not, American women are career oriented. I know in your culture that goes against the grain."

"What do you know about me and my culture?"

That 'got ya' look was back on his hawk-like face, like he suspected me of lying, maybe trying to con him. I wasn't about to slip up and tell him I had a dossier on him. "Arabic men are horribly old fashioned and domineering."

When his eyes glittered with irritation, I smiled. It wasn't hard to push his buttons. I swirled the sponge over his abs and moved on to his cock.

"Sorry you don't approve," he said tightly.

I sank down to my knees on the shower's stone floor driven by the undeniable need to taste him. That I'd never even considered doing this before didn't matter. He was different.

"I didn't say it was all bad," I said looking up at him.

The burning look in his eyes and the rigid set of his body told me he was holding back, waiting for me to make the next move. The sense of feminine power that filled me at that moment spurred me on.

"The domineering part can be fun at times," I murmured, smiling up at him.

I watched a nerve in his tight jaw pulse, made a yummy noise, and focused on his cock. It was hard bobbing in front of my face. I experimentally flicked my tongue out to taste him. Salty, sweet, and all man...mine. "It's even better than I imagined."

He shuddered.

A drop of pre cum glistened on his slit and I lapped it up, stealing it. He hissed in response making me quiver, emboldening me. I smiled, swirling my tongue around his hot cock's velvety head and then opened my mouth to take him in. His groan excited me, made me suck on him hard trying to take more of him in.

"Enough," he gritted out, his hands on my shoulders.

I gave him a frown, my lips still holding him trapped, but his tender look made me stop. I let him slip from my mouth and left him with a kiss and a promise. I wanted more. He pulled me up off the floor and my arms went around his neck. I kissed him ravenously knowing he tasted his essence on my tongue, reveling in it. I sucked on his tongue enflamed.

"Wrap your legs around my waist, Honor," he demanded.

I didn't need more encouragement. I wrapped my legs around his toned middle, my ass pressed against his burning erection, and I whimpered. He lifted me, thrusting into my pussy, and I cried out, my body clamping onto his huge cock. "Oh lord, that feels so good..."

"Call me Alex," he ordered.

"Alex," I said with a pleasured sigh as he thrust into me time and again. He groaned muttering love words I didn't understand but felt to the bottom of my soul. He backed me against the cool tiles as he fucked me hard.

17

My sex tightened even more than before, clinging to his driving cock as he plunged into me. I clung to him almost afraid to let go, wondering if I could take it, take him. And then he kissed me, driving high and hard inside me, and ground against me. I shattered, my pussy milking him, making him groan.

"Honor," he shouted, coming high and hard inside me.

Chapter Two

Alex snuggled up to the beautiful thief in his bed gazing down at her full breasts topped with hard pink nipples reddened from his attentions, the flare of her hips, and her creamy fragrant sex hidden by a thicket of gold curls. She wasn't the first thief that had ever tried to hijack his jewels but she was definitely the most bewitching.

In the past he'd dealt with thugs and cool calculating seductresses, not blushing almost-virgins. He felt like papa bear finding goldilocks in his bed. Instead, he'd found the pretty liar rifling his room. His gaze fell to his shaving kit on the dresser. He didn't need to look inside to know that Athena's necklace was gone. Fate had thrown a bewitching complication in his path.

Whatever she was, she wasn't a professional courtesan. Her delightful inexperience was enough to rouse his cock yet again. She also wasn't a professional thief. So, what the hell was she, and better still, why was she here gracing his bed?

The lady was a mystery; one he intended to explore fully. What should her punishment be for trying to rob him, he wondered with a smile. A weekend fulfilling all his sexual whims would suit him.

When she woke and her big blue eyes opened, he waited for her reaction. Would she come clean now? Her sultry gaze swept over him making him rock hard in an instant. Shit.

He'd been celibate too long; that had to be the reason she affected him so. Then her gaze flicked to the clock and she gasped slipping out of his grasp and leaping from his bed. His jaw tightened as she tried to run from him.

"Going somewhere?" he asked, stalking his prey with his eyes as she grabbed her clothes. She held her dress in front of her luscious breasts hiding them from him and he scowled.

"Well actually I was only paid for a short...um, I've got to go."

He shook his head. "The ferries gone by now, Honor. Surely my brother told you that when he hired you."

She frowned. "Well, I'll wait on the beach for the next one."

"For two nights. It doesn't run on the weekends." He watched the growing suspicion on her angelic face. She didn't trust him one bit; outside of bed that was. The feeling was mutual.

She stood fast clutching her dress. "But it doesn't say that in the schedule."

"Misprint," he said with a shrug watching her bite her lip. "Come back to bed, concubine. I want you again."

"What if I don't want you?" she said, her gaze lingering on his cock.

He watched her bite her lip in reaction, saw a blush heat her face, and his cock throbbed in reaction. Her arousal was as easy to read as her distrust of him.

It annoyed him, frustrated him, and made him want her even more. "I don't believe you, Honor. You were hired to fulfill all my sexual desires, unless you're lying about why you're here."

"I'm not the liar here," she said, her chin rising a notch.

"Good," he said, wondering what lies she was alluding to. So far he'd been up front with her; except that it wasn't his birthday, and he sure as hell knew she wasn't from his brother. But when confronted by a hot number like her, a man had to fight fire with fire. He stroked his cock seeing the hungry look in her eyes. "Come back to bed. I'll let you taste me again if you're good."

Her gaze flicked to the growing darkness outside the window and she sighed.

His heart stopped when she turned back to him with a shy smile and dropped her clothes. She walked toward the bed, her moves feline seductive and he held up a hand. "Stop."

She stopped in her tracks frowning at him. "What kind of game are you..."

He smiled at her frustration, enjoying her feisty attitude. "Play with yourself, love. I want to watch."

She sucked in a shocked breath. "I don't think..."

He locked gazes with her, not letting her look away. "For me."

Her hands moved up to cup her breasts, her fingers fanning her nipples as she gasped.

Alex bit back a groan as he watched His cock throbbed in reaction. He wanted everything from her, total surrender. Damned witch, what was she doing to him? He watched as one of her hands crept down to play with her creamy sex and her hips arched out at him.

He drank in the moan that poured out of her sexy mouth wanting to kiss her again. He wanted to taste her all over and he would before the night was through; his body hardened even more at the thought. It was all he could do not to reach out and take her but he wanted to teach her that he was master.

Little gasps came out of her mouth, and her legs trembled. She was close to coming. "Stop," he commanded. Her blue eyes snapped open in shock.

"But I need to..."

"I know what you need, bad girl. Come here." His gut twisted while he waited for her to decide whether to come on his command or run. When she walked to him with a tremulous smile on her lips, he breathed again.

The moment she came in range he pulled her into bed, pressing her back onto the mattress, his hand gliding to her creamy sex. He pressed her clit with his thumb saying, "Come now."

He groaned as she came on command. Her sex rippling like the ocean waves outside his window, her honey covering his fingers. He had to feel that inside her now. Before he could even think, he rolled onto his back and pulled her astride him.

Her sultry eyes widened at the change of position and then she smiled mounting him. Reveling in her surrender, he grasped her hips and thrust up into her filling her completely. He groaned when her sheath clung to him. She was so tight, a perfect fit. He gazed up at her beautiful face marveling that she was in his bed. Wondering why she'd tried to rob him.

Then he put those thoughts aside as he gave into his lust and thrust into her deep time and again until she was mewling. He drank in the sounds of her passion loving them. His balls tightened and his cock grew as she wet the head of his cock. He stroked the puckered rose of her ass and she let out a shocked gasp.

He slipped a finger lubricated with her juices into her back portal and she cried out, her ass and pussy convulsing as she came, wringing his orgasm from him. He followed her into bliss shooting his seed against her cervix.

She collapsed against him with a sigh their bodies still intimately joined.

Alex caught her to him with a growl. She was his and he was keeping her; at least until he learned all her secrets. His sultry captive. Satisfied and dazzled he held her fast when she started to rise.

"Stay put," he ordered gruffly.

"Somebody's grumpy," she teased, nibbling his ear.

Alex's cock throbbed anew as her teeth closed on his earlobe. The little thief wanted to play with him but she had a lot to answer for.

His hands slicked down her supple back to cup the sexy globes of her ass. He drew back a hand giving her three sharp spanks and groaned when her cunt tightened around him and she cried out in pleasure.

"Don't try to run from me again or I'll have to punish you," he said, shocked at his own words but knowing he meant them. He couldn't let her get away; after all, he had to know who was behind this plot to steal the showpiece from his spring collection.

The upcoming showing was the high point of his business year and he had to protect his business, his string of exclusive jewelry stores. It was a family firm actually, his sister Athena a designer, his brother Mike in charge of promotions, while he handled the dull business details. Honor ground against him, her sex milking him as he gave her one last spank, making him hard.

Chapter Three

The sound of birds singing woke me as the sun was rising. Alex's cock pressed against my ass, stiffening with a growing morning erection. I rubbed against him tantalized as his cock slipped between my legs, amazed by my renewed lust.

Alex grumbled in his sleep, his hand tightening on my breast, making me gasp. My nipple instantly hardened against his hot palm, and a brush fire of arousal rushed through me. I needed to run away, I knew it, but I couldn't stop myself from rubbing my creamy sex against his hot erection. The tip brushed my tingling clit making me quiver as I dry humped him.

I wanted another little souvenir to take with me before I left. I wanted him. My hand stole down to my stiff little clit, as I pleasured myself against him. I stifled my orgasmic cry in my pillow, shuddering as I came.

Drifting back down to earth, I snuggled against Alex, knowing he'd somehow turned me into a sex maniac overnight. I gloried in my new sexual awakening, wondering how many times in a row he could make me come.

I swept a fascinated gaze around his tiny villa in the light of day. My appraisal didn't take long. His place was miniscule, but clean and cozy featuring a small kitchenette, a sofa, and the big bed I now shared with him. His body heat warmed me, while his cock still throbbed against me, reminding me that while I might have gotten off on him he hadn't had the same pleasure. I had the urge to press back against him, or better yet, roll him over and do him properly.

My clothes still lay on the floor where I'd dropped them after he'd ordered me to play with myself. Just the memory made my nipples harden, my pulse racing, as a blush rushed through my body.

How could he have changed me so much in one short night? But I knew the truth, I'd changed myself, I'd needed this interlude to pull me out of the sexless rut I'd been in. At least I knew I wasn't frigid anymore, although the thought of being with another man didn't do a thing for me.

My tote bag still lay on the floor, undisturbed, a vivid reminder that I'd yet to complete my mission. I couldn't stir up any enthusiasm for the job that'd seemed so important yesterday. Even the twenty grand didn't have the power to motivate me. I'd found something so much better.

My crazy hormones said that I should stay put, sample my sexy sheik's lovemaking technique, while the common sense part of me that had driven my life for the last ten years screamed run. I was smart enough to admit that I'd been lucky so far; he hadn't caught me with the necklace.

All I had to do was slip out of his bed quietly, and run away. The ferry would be here at noon. I could make it. I knew he made up that crap about the ferry not running on the weekend. I'd checked the timetable myself. Misprint my eye. I'd given in and stayed the night because I wanted to not because my would-be sheik told me to.

I started to ease away from him and his hand tightened around my breast holding me fast. I bit back a groan. Maybe running away wouldn't be the piece of cake I'd thought it would be. I went still waiting breathlessly until I felt him relax against me, his grip on my breast loosening.

Very carefully, I lifted his hand, and eased out of bed, holding my breath when he stirred a little. He'd threatened to punish me if I left. It would be almost worth it to stick around for another one of his sexy spankings, but I told myself to get real.

There was no way I could stay and be his concubine, even if a big part of me ached to. Keeping a wary eye on my slumbering sheik, I slipped on my dress, grabbed my shoes, and picked up my tote bag. I wouldn't push my luck by putting on underwear. Instead, I left my bra and panties on the floor, a little souvenir for him to remember me.

I glanced back at Alex drinking him in once more, memorizing him. My gaze swept down his powerful swarthy body, to his rugged yet handsome face, to his raven dark hair. He was magnificent...unforgettable. He'd be a fiery memory on cold winter nights.

My nipples puckered inside my dress, my sex got instantly wetter, and my lips tingled for his kisses. What I wanted to do was crawl back into his bed and taste him again. Well hell, he'd thoroughly corrupted me, I decided, closing the door and running away.

Chapter Four

Alex watched her go through slitted eyes, and let out a sigh. The little sneak was still out to rob him. Maybe if he fucked her until she couldn't walk she'd behave. Hell, what he'd said about the ferry not running was true, she couldn't get far, but she could get hurt.

Didn't she know that coral could cut her tender feet and she'd blithely ran off barefoot? He rolled out of bed with a growl and slipped on board shorts and tennis shoes. A glance at her pink bra and panties still lying on his floor made him swell with need inside his suddenly too tight shorts. Damn it all.

With a grumble, he followed her footprints across the sand finding she attempted to hide her tracks as if that could stop him. He was pissed, he was horny, and he wanted satisfaction, now. And a few honest answers would be nice as well.

As expected, she was headed for the dock, taking what looked like the easiest path on the beach but actually treacherous and rocky. He resolutely tracked her through the village consisting of a few small cottages, which members of his mother's family owned, surrounding a fishing pier.

Only a few souls were out. He nodded at his cousin, Nick the gendarme and only lawman on the island, and kept going. Honor's eyes widened with shock when he stepped up onto the dock.

The little fool was still carrying her shoes and he glanced at her feel relieved to see they weren't bleeding. His possessive gaze swept up her body, taking in her skirt swirling around her long sexy legs, the feminine flare of her hips, and the tempting thrust of her breasts. He watched her nipples harden with satisfaction. At least he knew she wasn't lying about her sexual response to him.

"It's just the wind making me hard," she snapped.

He didn't believe that for a second. He walked toward her causing her to back up. Her apprehension made him smile. "I told you what I'd do to you."

She glanced around the vacant pier and then glared at him. "I don't have to obey you. I'm not your concubine anymore. I quit."

He smirked admiring her courage. "Wanna bet?"

She backed away. "What are you doing?"

31

He grabbed her tote bag, lifted out the necklace, and smiled. "Follow me back to the villa if you want this." Her outraged squeak as he turned to walk away made him chuckle.

"Stop thief," she called out.

"That's my line," he said over his shoulder.

"He's a jewel thief," she called out to the constable.

Alex smiled and nodded at Nick.

"Trouble here?" Nick asked, glaring at Honor.

"Yes there's trouble," she said. "He's the international jewel thief Ali Baba. Arrest him."

Alex froze as his childhood nickname rolled off her tongue. He bit back a groan as the last piece of the puzzle fell into place. Honor really was a gift from his practical joke loving brother. No, make that a matchmaker, or at least a sexual liaisons arranger.

Only Michael used his childhood nickname. And his brother said he was set in his ways, that he needed to get laid and stop moping since Risa dumped him last year. Hell, he'd moved on and he wasn't carrying a torch anymore except maybe for the blond who'd tried to rob him.

32

He turned to gaze at her stubborn little face as she glared up at the constable. He leaned back against the wall letting Jose face her wrath. He hadn't lied the ferry wasn't running, and there were no hotels. She'd have to stay with him. It seemed Honor wasn't a thief but she'd still have to be spanked.

"Well, aren't you going to do something?" she demanded.

Nick's eyes twinkled as he turned to him. "You want I should lock her up, *adelphos*?"

"Brothers?" she said with a gasp.

So she spoke Greek, at least she hadn't come here totally unprepared. Alex ignored her as she muttered and sauntered over to his laughing cousin. Within hours, he knew the news of this would be all over the island. "Maybe later."

"I can't believe it, the island cops are in your gang."

Gang? Alex wondered what kind of convoluted story Michael had given her. It was better this way. At least Honor wouldn't be after him for his money, like Risa had, he thought darkly. She'd be fucking him because she desired him.

He idly thought about putting her through the loyalty test that he and his cousins had made up in their

33

teens to weed out unsuitable women and rejected the notion. He hadn't played that game for years, although he knew the others still did, and he wasn't about to start now.

Yeah, but if he had with Risa he might have found her out before she screwed around on him and almost ruined his business. He shook off the thought already knowing that Honor was playing games. What he didn't know was how much it would cost him.

"For now I'm going to take it out in trade." Her outraged growl made him laugh. He walked away, calling over his shoulder, "Coming?"

"Yes, you bastard," she hissed. "I have to complete my mission. I'm not letting that necklace out of my sight."

"Good."

"Ouch," she cried out.

He stopped with a frown at her cry of pain and spun around to see her rubbing her foot. "Put your shoes on, Honor. I'll wait."

She glared back at him. "Don't order me around, you thieving gigolo."

His lips twitched at the name. That Mike had labeled his workaholic older brother a gigolo was the ultimate jest. But Honor really believed it. In a way, it made him want to live up to her expectations. Her stubbornness was exasperating as well as refreshing. He was used to women falling all over themselves in order to snag him for a husband.

"Would you rather cut your feet on the rocks?"

She muttered under her breath.

Alex watched her balance on one foot, tits jiggling as she bent to put her sandals on. The pink leather sandals weren't much protection but he'd keep her barefoot and in bed most of the weekend.

"I'm ready," she said straightening up.

He watched her face flame as she caught him admiring her shapely form. Her pink tongue flicked out to lick her lip and he remembered how it had looked wrapped around his cock in the shower. She hadn't wanted to let him go.

His cock grew inside his board shorts, and he noticed her hungry gaze linger on it.

Good, at least they were on the same page in bed. "This way," he said, leading her on an overland path to his cottage.

Chapter Five

I followed Alex on a new winding uphill path to his villa. For all I knew he could be leading me astray, but I trusted him on some level not to harm me. Mess with my sanity yes, turn me inside out with frustrated desire absolutely, but he wouldn't kill me. My mind a swirl of mixed emotions I struggled to keep up with his pace, breathing a little hard with my exertions.

This might be a short cut and easier on my feet but it was an uphill climb. To my displeasure he seemed to be having no trouble at all, his movements easy and strong, his sexy butt flexing as he climbed.

The man had the best butt I'd ever ogled, and ogle it I did as I followed him. The tingle that went through me as I recalled our night together was highly unprofessional but real. I wanted him again. And he hadn't lied about the ferry being shut down for the weekend. Maybe he was redeemable. I had to try. Besides, I didn't have much choice but to stick around.

How was it possible that he knew I had the necklace? I thought I'd been so clever, shown a real flair for skullduggery like my old man. Instead, I'd been caught red handed. Had he known all along, played games with me? The possibility infuriated me. Didn't he know he was in so much trouble? Didn't he care? The policeman I'd met was his brother, so it explained why he thought he was above the law, but if the Athens police or Interpol got involved he was dead meat.

Suddenly, it became clear why my client hadn't come for the necklace herself. She knew I was walking into a trap. "You can't get away with this you know," I called out a little breathlessly.

"I already have," he called out over his shoulder.

I kept my scornful gaze pinned to the perfect v of his powerful body and my blood heated despite my anger. He was a swarthy Adonis and my newly awakened sensuality was putty in his hands, damn it. He had the best ass I'd ever laid eyes on.

We started down the hill as his villa came into sight. I stumbled, crying out as my ankle turned and he instantly spun to catch me, the fast movement catching me by surprise. I gasped as his strong hands spanned my waist holding me fast and I melted as I gazed into his brown eyes. God, I was falling for him hard.

"Easy. I've got you."

The sensual rumble of his voice washed through me making me throb. I bit my lip as he half tugged me down the jagged steps to his courtyard. A few fishing boats bobbed in the sparkling waters of the Mediterranean, and birds sang in the olive trees, but I only had eyes for him. He was going to be firm with me; I could read it in the resolute look in his eyes. And to my shame, I welcomed his dominance. He picked me up, swinging me off the step to place me square in the middle of his courtyard. A wooden bench sat under an olive tree.

I gasped when he sat on the bench and tugged me over his knee. My soft belly and sensative mound landed on his hard lap and raging hard on, caused me to let out a little shriek instantly guessing his intention. "Hey..."

"I told you I'd punish you if you ran out on me," he said, flipping up my skirt baring my naked bottom. Why had I left my underwear behind? It would have at least given me some protection.

The sun warmed my backside and I blushed with mortification. I would have wiggled away but his arm around my waist held me fast. Then his big hand smacked down on my bottom making me cry out.

38

Heat spread throughout my bottom, making my clit stiffen and my sex ripple. Damn him. He kept up the stinging blows until I was arching back at him, whimpering with the need tightening inside me.

I moaned as each spank drove my clit against his leg. Breathless, on the verge of coming, I clung helplessly to him when he nudged my thighs apart and spanked my mound. I shrieked, coming hard, grinding myself against his firm hand.

He pulled me up to sit astride him, handling me like a rag doll, making my head spin. I gasped as my bare pubes pressed against the hard on in his shorts, and I arched mindlessly against him. I needed...

Then he slipped my sundress off over my head, stripping me, bringing me out of my orgasmic haze. Sunshine licked my body, reminding me that I was naked in public. What if the fishermen had witnessed my spanking?

"Stop," I said half-heartedly, but my dress was already on the sand. I gazed into Alex's sultry eyes, both angry and turned on. My face heated, probably as red as my ass, I thought forlornly, and I glared back at him.

It wasn't fair that he was turning me into a sex addict. It also wasn't fair that I was naked in public while he remained covered up and hidden from my hungry gaze.

"Talk to me, Honor. If that is your real name," he commanded.

I shivered recognizing the suspicion in his voice and didn't like it; I wasn't the liar around here. "Of course it's my real name. I don't lie." I snapped but I had deceived him and it went against my own personal code.

"Tell me about your client."

I shrugged. There was no need to keep secrets and maybe if I told him it would convince him to go straight. "The Countess," I said with an edge to my voice and noticed the startled look on his face.

Apparently, he hadn't been expecting her to seek retribution. He'd probably thought her husband had hired me. I wouldn't be jealous of his former lover, I told myself firmly. I'd only glimpsed the haughty brunette before I'd dealt with her lawyer. Were his eyes twinkling? If this was some kind of kinky love game of theirs, I'd kill him.

"Describe her," he said.

I wriggled against the firm arm he had wrapped around my waist, and gasped when it only succeeded in

40

grinding my tingling sex against his erection. His quick indrawn breath told me he was hurting, too. Good. I wanted him to feel as wild and frustrated as I did.

"Stop that," he said, giving me a spank.

I glared back at him, my pussy rippling as my bottom burned. I ached for him to touch me again, which was really crazy. "Short, brunette, and icy."

"Ah," he said, leaning back against the tree.

I frowned at him. Did he have that many conquests that he couldn't keep them straight? He tilted his head, studying me like I was the most fascinating creature alive, making me squirm inside.

"And you don't do this kind of gumshoe work for a living?"

That was the understatement of a lifetime. At least I had the satisfaction of knowing I intrigued him. "What was your first guess?" I said with a smile, relaxing. It was actually nice to be sunbathing naked and the hunk holding tight to me made me drool.

"The way you kissed me. Like you meant it."

His confident statement made my smile falter. Was I that transparent? "So sue me. I'm not a pro. I'm being paid well to retrieve the necklace. Then I'll rejoin the rest of my party from the museum, fly back home, and get on with the rest of my life."

"So you're not traveling alone?"

"I accompanied a collection to the Athens Museum. I'm more of a gofer for the Director. I had some time on my hands, was made this startling offer, and here I am."

"Your boss just lets you go off on your own?"

"He doesn't own me, despite his wishes to the contrary."

"What?"

"I don't want to spoil the moment by talking about Hal." At his intrigued glance, I hurried to change the subject. There was no way I wanted to discuss the museum director who wanted to marry me even though he thought I was a dud in bed. "It's not too late to go straight you know. You're a smart capable, man you could have a real job, not be a gigolo." His amused expression made me mad.

"Are you trying to save me?"

"Yes." I wondered at his startled smile but then he kissed me and my thoughts fled. I kissed him back moaning into his mouth when he tugged on my nipples. I arched my pussy against him, so close to coming.

Then his hand slipped between my legs to touch my clit. He tugged at it making me scream. As I came I realized he hadn't been satisfied. He was holding out on me. When he pulled me off his lap to stand on wobbly legs before him I could only look at him bemused.

Honor Blackwell did not stand around in her birthday suit while a dominant hunk ogled her. But that was the old me, the new me seemed to be putty in his capable hands. His playful swat made me stick my tongue out at him.

"Go get our shower started. I'll join you in a few minutes."

I went, abandoning my bag, the necklace, and my clothes, my warped mind looking forward to his joining me for some water fun.

Chapter Six

Alex waited until the bewitching blond went inside his hideaway to reach for her tote bag. His stiff cock throbbing with each rapid heartbeat, reminding him that she was leading him around by his dumb handle. He had to learn her secrets.

Her story was intriguing, astounding, and just kooky enough to be true. Trust his brother to send him an unusual beauty. But could Honor live up to her name, could she really be trustworthy?

He rummaged through her bag, relieved to find handcuffs and mace inside. He smiled as he pushed them aside and reached for her wallet. At least she hadn't rushed into this caper totally unprotected.

He glanced at her ID, a Wisconsin driver's license, and then pulled out her passport to see if they matched. They did, but they didn't tell him a great deal only that she hadn't traveled much; her passport had only two entries. At least she hadn't lied to him about her name. Her wallet contained little else, a credit card, little cash, and, most importantly, no photos of other lovers.

He remembered her reaction to talk about her boss, Hal. The idea of another man touching her made him crazy. Who was this Hal guy, and what had he tried that made her so defensive?

Sunlight bounced off a silver colored satellite phone at the bottom of her bag. It matched the ones his company Crown Jewelers used for business. Michael must have given it to her knowing that regular cell phones didn't work out here.

He flipped through the contacts noticing she had the American embassy and Michael on speed dial. Smart girl. There was also a third number on speed dial. Probably Hal he surmised with a scowl. He rolled his shoulders forcing himself to relax and punched his brother's number.

"Mike Lawler attorney at law."

Alex scowled at his brother's greeting, confirming his suspicions. Michael knew the call was coming from Honor's phone. "What kind of game are you playing now, Mike?"

"Alex. I wasn't expecting to hear from you. How are things in babe land?" Michael said with a chuckle.

Alex sighed knowing his brother saw through his bluster. "Tell me all about Honor."

"So I take it that you got my gift."

His brother's gleeful tone made him roll his eyes. It had been a long time since they'd shared sexual secrets and lovers. "It's not my birthday."

"I know. She's your pull her head out of your ass, stop moping, and get on with your life present."

Alex knew he was referring to the debacle with Risa and refused to rise to the bait. He wasn't pining for her. Hell, he knew now that he'd never even loved her.

She'd been suitable, both sides of his squabbling family had liked her, and she'd been understanding when he'd put work first. He should have known it was because she had something going on the side. When she'd run off with one of his biggest competitors it'd almost been a relief. "Who says I was moping? Was Athena in on this?"

"Not exactly. And don't sound so disapproving, our kid sister is a grown woman now, she could handle the truth."

"Asshole," Alex said and smiled, relaxing.

"Takes one to know one, adelphos."

"Tell me about Honor."

"Ah, Honor. She's an artist, apparently not a very good one, according to her mentor and employer. She

46

accompanied a collection from the University of Wisconsin to the museum. I saw her and everything clicked."

He didn't like his brother's appreciative tone even though it was lighthearted. And he found it hard to believe that Honor wasn't good at anything she was that passionate about. He felt very territorial about this woman for the short while he's known her. Now he understood why some of his uncles still kept Harems. "It better not have."

Michael laughed. "Man you've got it bad. She must be better than I figured. Don't worry, I didn't make a move on her. Although why you don't like to share anymore..."

"So how'd you hire her away from her mentor?"

"When she found out that he had planned a little rendezvous for them she was pissed. Told him only her vibrator got her off, kicked him in the balls, and insisted on separate rooms. I met Hal when he was in the bar drowning his sorrows and icing down his balls. After I bought him a beer, he got rather chatty. I set up a little adventure for her. You can thank me later."

"What'd you offer her?"

"Twenty grand. It seemed like a fortune to her apparently. She kept muttering about being able to quit her part-time jobs and work on her collection."

His mind boggled. "Like she's got the qualifications to do PI work, how'd she have the guts to even try it?"

"Actually, she does have the qualifications. It's the family business that and psychic readings."

"What?"

"Hal got pretty loose lipped when I bought him a beer. Her old man's a PI. Low level cases mostly. Mother runs a tourist trap in a resort town and tells fortunes on the side."

"I want you to collect her things from the hotel and then make a drop. I'll have an order waiting at Madame Helena's."

"You're keeping her?"

The shock in his brother's voice made him smile. "Oh yeah. If anyone asks the ferry's broken down and waiting for a part."

"Until when?"

"Until further notice."

Chapter Seven

My legs were practically boneless as I enjoyed Ali's; make that Alex's, state of the art shower. Body jets hit my nipples making them tingle. Hell, my whole body was tingling. Who knew being spanked could be so erotic.

The scent of sandalwood, the warm water caressing my body all reminded me of the delights to come. But why was he taking his time? I rinsed the sandalwood body wash off my body wondering why he hadn't joined me.

It was then that I heard the sound of a motorboat speeding away. I let out a cry of dismay. Was it possible he'd run out on me; escaped with the necklace? Of course, how stupid could I have been not to consider that possibility? I slapped off the shower and jumped out, skidding across the tile floors as I ran after him.

Here I'd been mooning over a brute who'd spanked me and he'd tricked me. Shit, he also had access to my passport, and the mace my dad gave me. He could have taken everything and left me stranded.

I tore open the villa's front door and sprinted outside naked. A glance at the bench told me my clothes and bag were missing. Damn. Tears misted my eyes. I'd really started to trust him. I turned to run toward the beach, and froze when I saw Alex trudging toward me, a determined look on his face. His aggravated expression said he'd read my doubts of him and he didn't like it.

Tough, all thieves were liars and I wasn't going to trust him. The speedboat skimming across the water, and the duffle bag he carried told their own story. He'd had the bag delivered, could have sent me back. Why was I so glad that he hadn't? I knew a goofy smile curved my lips but I couldn't help it. He hadn't left me.

Still, there was the matter of my missing things. "Where are my clothes?"

"I prefer you nude, Honor," he said when he reached me, cupping my breast, fanning the nipple with his rough fingertip.

I whimpered leaning into him. "You can't keep me naked," I protested weakly.

"Concubines are often kept nude to prevent their escape."

I glared at him hearing the resolve behind his teasing tone. He liked me naked. He was keeping me. At least for now. My face heated, even as my sex pulsed, my honey flowing. How could he do this to me with just a look? "Who was that?" I asked, looking toward the speedboat now only a speck in the distance.

I noticed another smaller vessel tied off at the dock. I could steal it and escape. As if guessing the directions of my thoughts he frowned.

"Don't even think about it, Honor. I had one of my associates do a little shopping for you."

"For me?" I squeaked, pleased. "You bought me a present?"

He smiled and took my hand. "Several. Come inside and I'll show you."

I walked beside him, holding his hand, overwhelmed. I should really leave; throw his gifts back at him but I didn't want to. "This isn't going to stop me from doing my duty."

"I know, you're a loyal little thing aren't you."

I peered up at him trying to see if he was teasing me but couldn't tell. He towed me toward the table and chairs and sat opening the first shopping bag. I tried to peer inside and blushed when he pulled out what looked like clip-on earrings, a short stubby dildo, and a tube of cherry flavored lube. It was as if he knew my secret fantasies.

My eyes widened when he drew me toward him and toyed with my nipples, rolling them in his fingers lengthening them. I gasped, sagging against him, my knees weakening.

"What are you doing to me?" I murmured out of my head. He unclipped one of the jewels, fastening it to my nipple. The ruby hung down tugging at my sensitive peak.

"Dressing my pretty love slave," he murmured. "These are nipple clamps guaranteed to make you crazy."

Shit, I was already there. I cried out when he toyed with my other nipple lengthening it before clamping on the other jeweled nipple clamp. I moaned, my sex pulsing, rubbing against him with fever. My fascinated gaze flicked to the dildo and tube of gel.

"I noticed how much you liked anal play last night," he said with a smile. "This is your butt plug." He picked up the devise. "Bend over, precious, and I'll let you try it out," he coaxed.

Blushing, my ass quivering, I did as he said, gasping when he stroked a lubricated finger along my crease teasing me. My pussy and ass pulsed. I pushed them back toward him. When his finger slipped inside my ass, I cried out. "Oh yes, take me there."

"Not until I think you're ready," he said firmly.

I cried out in protest when he withdrew his teasing finger but then gasped when he pressed the well-lubricated butt plug against my ass and I froze. Suddenly, it felt big and I got a little nervous when he pressed it into me, tensing.

"Relax, love, I won't do anything you don't beg me for," he said with a chuckle.

I moaned, embarrassed at the reminder that I'd begged him to take my ass, and knowing that I'd no doubt do it again.

Then he started to ease it into me and I gasped as my body rippled around the plug, adjusting to it. He waited a moment and then slowly pressed it inside me to the hilt, filling me completely.

I whimpered, sexually overcome as my ass and pussy clenched. How did he know that I'd toyed with myself there? He was awakening all kinds of forbidden sensations inside me.

"Up now," he said, straightening me.

I stood erect gasping as the butt plug went deeper and my anus rippled around it while my pussy quivered. I was close to coming, and he was still dressed and in complete control. I didn't like it.

But the sultry look in my sheik's eyes as I scowled at him told me he was far from uninvolved. And then there was the huge bulge of his hard on inside his shorts to consider. It was proof he wanted me.

"Sit," he said, picking me up and sitting me on the table.

I gasped as my ass touched the wooden tabletop, the plug moving inside me making me cream.

"Look at me," he said, capturing my jaw.

I gazed into his eyes, totally lost to passion, to his masterful touch. It was a new sensation, one I'd enjoy for the weekend. "Yes," I said softly.

"I spoke with your employer."

His words made me shiver. I wanted to die when I thought of him talking to Hal. What might he have said about me? That I was cold, had no talent? "Hal," I bit out angrily, aware Alex studied my reaction. So I hadn't had luck with men in general, still didn't if I was some gigolo's concubine.

"No," he said, shaking his head. A nerve pulsed in his jaw. "Although we should talk about him."

And then it hit me that he meant the Countess. I let out an appalled gasp and tried to wriggle away but Alex's big hand clamped to my hip held me fast.

"You called the countess," I said bitterly. Of course, he had. They probably played these sex games all the time and I was caught in the middle. I didn't like the raven arch of his brow, the speculative gleam in his eyes. He probably thought I was green with envy but I wasn't going to give him the satisfaction of appearing jealous.

"No. I called her representative." He casually pulled the necklace out of his short's pocket.

"Her attorney," I said, my eyes fixed forlornly on the necklace in his hands. The sunlight pouring through the windows refracted rainbows off the beautiful work of art but my heart was heavy. He was going to give it back to me and send me on my way. Mission accomplished so why did I feel like crying? I froze when he carefully put the necklace on me, the jewels instantly warming to my body heat, and cast a helpless look at his compelling face bracing myself for his dismissal. Instead, he smiled.

"It looks like it was made for you, beloved."

"But it wasn't, it was made for another. She employed me to get it back for her," I said, my heart sinking as I said the words. I blinked back the tears misting my eyes and tried to appear cool.

"She doesn't want the necklace back anymore. She wants me."

"Of course she does," I muttered, glaring at him, his words confirming that this was some kind of sex game of theirs. Well I didn't want to play.

"No. She wants you to turn me over to her. Betray me."

My jaw dropped as he said the words in a matter of fact tone that belied the tension in his body. What the hell could I say to that? I desperately needed the money...

"Well," he said, glancing at me. His finger toying with the jewel hanging from my nipple, making me gasp, my body trembling. "What would you rather have— the money or me?"

I couldn't speak for a moment overwhelmed. I needed the money but I couldn't do it to him even if he deserved it. But maybe it would do him good. Make him go straight."

"Right," he said, leaning forward to lap at my nipple.

I cried out as he laved my swollen bud making me shudder, the jewels tugging at my breasts.

"But...I didn't mean..." I started to protest.

"Never mind," he growled against my breast. "At least you can't lie to me about this."

His hand slipped between my legs homing in on my clit. I hissed with pleasure when he played with it, making it stand out. And then he was laying me back and bent to lap at my pussy. I cried out as his tongue swirled over me and my eyes rolled back in my head.

He sucked my clit into his mouth drawing hard on it, my pussy spasming, my ass milking the butt plug as I came. He stood surging into me with one fierce thrust filling me. I cried out at the double invasion. He growled, withdrew, and slammed into me again. He draped my legs over his shoulders pulling my hips off the table and took me hard, surging into me until I was breathless, my pussy gripping him, as I moaned.

"You're mine," he whispered, pinching my nipples.

"Yes," I whimpered, crying out as he tugged on my tortured nips, driving me higher.

"Say it," he demanded.

"I'm yours," I said, moaning when he spilled inside me.

Chapter Eight

Late that afternoon Alex cast a possessive look over Honor. She lay in his bed, sated, her nipples still a little red from the clamps. Her naughty toys lay in a shelf on his dresser and he'd enjoy introducing her to them all. He knew she'd betray him in the end but he'd get his fill of her first.

A little voice in his head said it wouldn't be that easy to tire of her. He couldn't get enough. She woke from her slumber to look at him with sultry eyes and smiled, spreading her legs to show him her jewels. His cock twitched even as his heart panged. Damn, how could he let her go?

"I've another gift for you," he said carrying another shopping bag to her. Her blush when she looked at the bag delighted him.

"More sex toys," she said, sitting up in bed.

He smiled at her unabashed reaction loving that sex made her cheerful as hell. She had a delightfully kinky side that he'd enjoy helping her explore. It was enough for now. He would keep her with sex for as long as he could.

"We can talk about them later," he said, watching her playful pout. "First, I've got another treat for you." He opened a drawstring on a black shopping bag and spilled out the contents on her lap. Art supplies, charcoals, a sketchpad, and pastels lay on her lap. She let out an excited whoop, giggling.

"That's the way to my heart, Alex, plenty of sketch paper," she said, snatching up the pad.

He smiled at her genuine gasp of delight. With most women, it would take diamonds to get such a reaction. "And here I thought that sex toys and spankings were the way to your heart."

Her eyes twinkled as she gazed up at him. "Those, too."

"I'll have to remember that." He groaned when she reached out to wrap her arms around his middle.

"Thank you," she said, hugging him tight.

Alex could barely breathe when she held him like that. "You're welcome." He gasped when her warm breath blew over his cock, instantly rousing him. The little minx was insatiable and he wouldn't have it any other way.

"But how did you know?

"You mentioned your art."

"I did?" she said with surprise.

"I was busy licking your cunt at the time."

"Ah, that's why I don't remember. I've never had any man do that for me before."

"Well then, the men you've dated are pricks," he said, hating the thought of her with another man.

"I agree." She flickered her tongue over his cock.

Alex groaned as she brought him to life. Her tongue swirled around his cock's head and flicked at the strand underneath. Then she dipped down to suck his balls. He let out a groan bracing his legs to keep from falling. She sucked him into her mouth drawing on him hard as she fisted his cock.

His balls grew tight and he knew he was close. He tried to pull her away but she wouldn't let go, sucking harder until he exploded shouting her name. She sucked him dry, drawing his cum from him, then let him go with a satisfied sigh.

She leaned back in bed gazing up at him with heat. "That's how I want to draw you, when you have that sultry satisfied look."

Alex looked down at her bemused. "Come," he said taking her hand. "It's time for my swim."

61

Chapter Nine

I picked up the sketchbook and charcoals he'd given me and followed my naked sheik outside. When his firm hand closed around mine, I knew I wasn't going anywhere. Being naked in public seemed as natural as breathing now, and I smiled when his sultry glance ran over me.

I did want to capture his fierce masculinity on paper. He spread a blanket on the beach and took the art supplies from me, dumping them on the spread.

I wouldn't betray him no matter how tempting the commission was. I'd just have to bite the bullet and take on another part time job to make extra money. I'd eventually achieve my goal of putting my debut showing together. In the mean time, I could sell the occasional painting at Sheri's new gallery.

I glanced at my sheik warmly, making up my mind to do my best to reform him before I left. I wouldn't betray him but I would return the necklace.

The return of her property would just have to satisfy the bitch. I couldn't help wondering what other women he'd had. A man in his profession no doubt had a past. For all I knew he'd left a string of ex wives behind him.

"Come on," he said, tugging me into the water with him. I went with a laugh as the sparkling waters swept over me, and I looked into his laughing eyes. He loved the water and he seemed to delight in me. It was enough.

"Can you swim?" he asked

"Like a fish," I said with a grin, remembering my summers at the lake. "I grew up next to a lake in Wisconsin Dells, a little tourist town."

"Good," he said, going into deeper water.

I luxuriated in the feeling of the warm sparkling water lapping around me, the feel of my sheik holding my hand. And then he pulled me into his arms, holding me afloat, and I pressed against him.

"Don't worry, I've got you."

"I think that's the other way around," I said, wrapping my arms around his neck and kissing him. He deepened the kiss, pulling my wet body against his, sweeping me off my feet. I clung to him, groaning, as I felt his cock stiffen against me. He was just as hungry as I was.

"Aren't you worried about sharks?" I teased.

He smiled. "I think I can hold my own with the predators of the deep."

"I expect that you can," I said, trusting him.

"Wrap your legs around me, concubine," he demanded.

I did, gasping when it brought my open sex into contact with his hot body. What was he doing to me? I let out a cry of delight when his hands tightened on my ass. Then he bent to kiss me, his hot mouth slanting over mine. He nipped my lower lip demanding access and I opened my mouth letting his tongue ravage me.

I moaned when his cock rubbed against me, and arched against him.

"Want me?" he teased, holding back.

I nipped his earlobe in revenge because he held out on me, and whimpered. "You know that I do, tease."

"Excellent," he said, surging into me with a growl.

I cried out, my sex spasming at the sudden invasion, while I held him tighter.

His hands, holding my ass, tightened as he drove into me time and again, making me quiver, my pussy rippling against him.

"Baby, you're killing me," he said with a growl.

The feeling was entirely mutual, I decided, moaning. I gazed into his hot eyes, melting as he took me hard. I was putty in his masterful hands, and I loved it.

He gripped my ass tighter, surging deeper into me, and my pussy tightened around him, milking his thrusting cock as I shuddered.

Everything tightened, and I exploded, sobbing with pleasure as I came. He held still, deep inside me, and growled as he came.

After a moment, Alex slowly let me go, disengaging our bodies. I gazed at him knowing I was in love with him, but also knowing I could never tell him. I was just a temporary diversion to him. My knees wobbled and I leaned against him, listening to the reassuring beat of his heart. His arms came around me to steady me.

"You okay?"

"Better than okay," I said, my body still sizzling. "I'm surprised we hadn't set fire to the water."

He tipped back his head and laughed. "Beloved, you are a refreshing delight. I'd better get you onto dry land," he said, taking my hand to stride through the water.

I walked out of the surf feeling happy. At least he found me delightful. I relaxed walking towards the blanket; water trickling off my body while the intense sun kissed me. It was heaven.

I smiled at my sheik, my hungry gaze glued to his fluid movements as he slicked the water off his beautiful nude form. He turned, catching me ogling him and smiled. My heart skipped a beat. I suddenly had to know about the competition. "Have you ever been married," I blurted out.

He smiled. "You're feeling territorial about me. I like it."

"So answer my question."

"Married, no. Engaged, yes."

I frowned not liking the idea of another woman having a prior claim on him.

"Her name was Risa, and she dumped me," he said flatly.

Was he still hung up on her, using me as a distraction? I gazed into his eyes but only saw irritation there. Risa had hurt his pride. "What happened?"

"The usual story. She found someone who suited her better. A wealthier guy who could offer her more."

I touched his arm. "I'm sorry about what she did but you're better off without her."

He smiled down at me. "I do believe you're right. You wouldn't marry a man for his money."

"Of course not," I said. This Risa person was a gold digger. She'd probably moved on to a more successful thief.

"What about you?" he asked. "Have you ever been married?"

The question took me by surprise. Did he suspect that I had a past, too? I smiled at him. "No. I've never been married. And you know about Hal. He's the only one who's ever proposed to me." Alex's hot gaze raked over me, making me tremble.

"Then those Wisconsin men must be blind."

Blushing, and pleased at the compliment, I picked up the sketchbook he'd bought me and started to work, wanting to capture him. Unfortunately, charcoals and paper couldn't begin to pick up all his essence but I was thrilled that he'd bought them for me.

He'd spent probably his little bit of spare cash on me. Having grown up poor, I knew just how much that meant. He cared for me.

"I wish I had a camera," I said with a sigh, glancing at my beautiful surroundings, the land and sea, the charmingly quaint tumbledown villa. "It'd be something I could take with me when I..." I turned to look at him, not wanting to finish my statement, to find him staring at me.

Would he regret our parting as much as I would? Probably not, I was just a temporary concubine. I didn't want to think about leaving just yet. This weekend I'd just have fun, enjoy my sheik. "This little speck in the Mediterranean is just so unbelievably beautiful"

"Don't you find my villa a little...primitive?" he asked.

"Like you," I said to lighten the mood. When he gave me a wicked smile I added, "Actually it reminds me of home. I grew up in a lake side cottage very much like this one." The startled look in his eye made me wonder if I'd passed some test.

"Be right back," he said, walking toward the villa.

"But I want to sketch you," I complained as my subject walked away. When he disappeared inside the villa, I knew it was the perfect opportunity to run, try to flag down one of the fishing boats, but I stayed put. I wasn't leaving without getting my fill of my sheik. I could catch the ferry on Monday and still make it back for my red eye flight home to the States.

When Alex came back a moment later, a beach bag slung over one powerful bare shoulder, an easel, canvas, and oil paints in his other hand; I let out a cry of delight. "My goodness, it looks like a complete traveling oil painting set. Where on earth did you have them stashed?" I asked as he set up the easel for me and then set up a folding table next to the easel.

"Athena left them behind last winter. I assume the oils will still be useable."

My excitement dulled a little at the mention of yet another rival, but I didn't let that stop me from oohing and ahhing as he opened up a case of professional quality set of supplies.

"They should be perfect," I said, throwing my arms around his neck. I pulled him down for a quick kiss, my happiness bubbling over. When I pulled away, there was a startled look on his handsome face. "Thank you."

The sultry smile he gave me made my knees weak, but as I studied his face, I knew I had to get busy and paint him. "I'd like you to pose for me."

He smiled. "Anything you say, Honor." "But first I think you might like to use this," he said, reaching into the beach bag to fish out a Nikon camera.

I let out a startled gasp when I caught sight of the expensive camera. "Wow. I wouldn't know which button to push," I said with a smile.

"Why not. You seem to have figured out which ones to push on me." He grinned.

I flashed a startled look up at him, trying to decide if he was teasing me. Was he feeling a little torn himself.

"All you do is point and click. Here, I'll show you," he said, taking a shot of my face.

I watched as he showed me how to check the image on the screen and I wasn't surprised to see the look of pure bliss on my face. He'd captured me in an interesting shade of light and shadow, my face glowing, sun shining off my nude body, as I'd smiled up at him. He was rapidly turning me into a wanton woman. What did surprise me were the serious skills he'd displayed. "You're really good at that."

"Photography is a hobby of mine," he said.

"You know you could make a living at that," I said, gazing up at him as the thought crystallized. Here was a way for him to go straight.

"Do you really think so?"

His non-committal reply wasn't very encouraging but I had to try. "Of course, Athens would be a gold mine for a man with your talent."

"You mean taking snapshots of the tourists," he said with a half smile.

His amused, almost indulgent tone, made me see red. "It's an honest living," I snapped back stung by his attitude. I'd grown up catering to the tourist trade.

"You're right." He nodded and pulled me into his arms.

I squirmed a little in his embrace wondering if he was just humoring me. Then his arms tightened around me and he bent to kiss me, driving thoughts of rebellion from my mind. I burned as his hot lips brushed across mine and kissed him back suddenly boneless as I leaned against him. When he pulled away, I gazed into his smoldering eyes, feeling dazzled.

"I'm sorry for being insensitive."

His words made me wonder how he knew his comment would bother me. It was almost like he knew my background but that was impossible. We were just so attuned to one another that he read my emotions, I decided with a smile.

I leaned against him warmed by his softened attitude, knowing I'd overreacted. "And I'm sorry for making such a big deal over it."

He nodded, letting me go, thrusting the camera into my hands. I took it from him surveying the local for things I wanted to capture. While it was charming, only one thing seemed vitally important. I wanted to take Alex with me. I turned and snapped several shots of him catching him by surprise.

If he could take nude pictures of me, I wanted the same privilege with him. I waited for him to complain but instead he just leaned back against the olive tree and posed, letting me shoot several more pictures of him. After I was satisfied that I'd captured him from all angles, I turned to take photos of the hillside and villa, and finally the sparkling Mediterranean. Then I handed the camera back to him.

He flashed me that indulgent smile again but this time I didn't take umbrage. I felt pretty darned indulgent when it came to him. "Thank you for the use of your camera! I'd better get to painting before I lose the light."

He nodded and opened up a bottle of sparkling water, setting it on the table he'd set up next to the easel.

"Drink first. Don't forget to keep hydrated," he scolded. "You're not used to these conditions."

I nodded, properly chastened, and took a cooling drink to satisfy him. He nodded and opened up a bottle of sunscreen, slathering me with lotion. I stood there as he fussed over me, feeling cosseted, like I was more to him than just a temporary concubine. It was a dangerous fantasy, one I couldn't afford to give in to. Finally, he popped a floppy white hat on my head, and stood back to study me.

"How do you want me?" he asked.

Any way I could get you, I thought with a smile, wondering if I could convince him to come home with me, but I knew he was talking about his pose. "Just get comfy," I said, and smiled when he sat down on the blanket and gazed right at me, one of his knees raised.

Sunlight glistened off his deeply tanned body, and his cock was semi-hard and nestled against his thigh. I practically drooled but forced myself to refocus. The man definitely wasn't shy about his magnificent body and I needed to capture it for posterity.

"Perfect," I said and picked up a brush. As I began to paint I went into my own world, and everything else seemed to fade away. My brush fairly flew and I realized that I was painting with a whole new fluidity I hadn't had before. There was nothing tentative about it as my creativity was unleashed. I knew I had Alex to thank for my new uninhibited style. He'd turned me into a loose woman.

Chapter Ten

Alex lay back watching the woman he was rapidly falling for paint him. Her voluptuous body glistening from the sun screen he'd coated her with, her blond hair tumbling out of the silly floppy hat he'd put on her.

Honor was completely focused on her art, it reminded him of his single-minded focus when it came to business. She was trying to reform him, save him from a life of crime. Her sweet efforts touched his heart.

Could he trust her with the truth, or would it destroy the fantasy for her?

There was another reason for keeping up the illusion; it was a way of keeping up walls, not being susceptible to his desire for her. If he kept things as they were, he'd be in control. He idly wondered how long he could keep her captive. The sun was beginning to set when she put down her brush and stepped back to gaze at her canvas.

He stood, feeling a little stiff from posing for so long, and walked over to her. When he gazed at the canvas, he went still, amazed by her natural talent.

According to what Hal had told his brother Michael, she was just a beginner, with a long way to go. "You're no amateur," he said, earning a startled smile from Honor. It confirmed that she wasn't used to having her work praised. "Whatever Hal has told you is a line of bull."

"Thanks," she said with a shy smile. "I already figured that out for myself, but I don't usually show my works to the public."

"That's going to change," he said, pissed that her supposed mentor was trying to squelch her growth as an artist.

"I know," she agreed, letting out a sigh. "I'm starting to put together a collection for my first showing. I have a friend named Sherri who's going to be opening a small art gallery in the Dells. She's going to feature regional and Native American artists, and she's agreed to give me a showing. That's why I agreed to come along on this trip with Hal, and also why I jumped at the chance to make a little money on the side."

He nodded, fully understanding what motivated her to take a risk to track him down. Even though he knew it was a risk, it was on the tip of his tongue to tell her who he really was and why he was holed up here. He was waiting for his cousins, and trusted curriers to pick up his stones.

However, he didn't want to ruin her fantasy. For a formerly modest woman, she was really getting off on being ravaged by a sheik. His cock started throbbing. He couldn't get enough of her.

Then Honor's stomach grumbled, and he smiled knowing she needed food more than sex now.

"Come on, it's time for dinner." He carefully picked up her wet canvas.

Then he waited for her to pack her paints, and then followed her into the cooling shade of the villa. The scent of the Moroccan stew he'd been heating perfumed the air.

Honor took a deep breath. "Something smells wonderful."

"Moroccan stew and pita bread, a mix of two cultures, just like me." Her quick gaze told him she was absorbing the information, trying to figure out what made him tick. "I started heating them when I came in for the camera and art supplies."

He carefully placed her painting in a quiet corner to dry and turned to see her smiling at him in approval and lost a little more of his heart.

"Come on," he said, a bit more gruffly than he intended, taking her hand and towing her toward the bathroom. "We've got to clean up and dress for dinner."

"Going formal are we?" she teased.

"Beloved, you have no idea," he said with heat, and pulled her into the shower. He had plans for her tonight. He was going to thoroughly enjoy her, maybe get her out of his system.

His cock throbbed when he lathered her, swirling the sponge around her sexy body, but he held himself back. He wanted to draw this out, make it last, make her crazy.

She moaned, pressing close, reaching out to wrap her hand around his cock.

He groaned as she captured him in a grip, his cock throbbing in her delicate hand. After a moment, he steeled his resolve and pulled away, giving her a quick spank in warning. "No more. Tonight you're my little slave girl and I give all the commands."

She pouted up at him, pressing her wet body against him. "You're a mean master to tease me this way."

"Love, you don't know what teasing is yet," Alex bit out as her tantalizing tits rubbed against his chest. She was going to kill him if she kept that up. He ran a firm hand over the curve of her sleek flanks telling himself that he was in charge. "My first command is that you can't come until I tell you to." He smiled when she sucked in a shocked breath.

"That's not fair," she complained. "It's barbaric making me come on command."

"Welcome to the stone age, love," he said with a smile. "Tonight you obey me."

She shivered, pressing against him. "You're going to drive me mad."

"Good, because you've already made me half-crazy," he said, his cock throbbing against her creamy mound. He switched off the shower before he gave into temptation and fucked her where she stood. Her grumble as he pulled away made him smile. He resolutely took her hand ignoring her rebellious glare and pulled her out of the shower, tossing her a towel. "Dry me."

She approached him with a glare, rubbing the towel over his stiff body, making him bite back a groan. He balled his hands at his sides to keep from touching her.

A natural concubine she did not make but he knew he'd never get enough of her. Tonight was all about teasing her, making her want him more. But he knew he was in serious danger of having things backfire on him. When she rubbed the towel over his cock he groaned and pulled away. "Enough. Now it's your turn."

"Okay," she said with a smile.

Her sudden change of attitude made him smile. She trembled when he touched her, gently rubbing the towel over her body, her nipples hardening instantly. He rubbed the towel over them again and she leaned toward him.

He moved down to dry off her mound and throbbed when he cupped her creamy heat in his hand. He couldn't resist brushing her stiff little clit making her gasp.

He dropped the towel not wanting to push his luck and took her hand. "Come on," he said, towing her back to the bedroom.

He opened the dresser drawer and pulled out the hot pink bustier he'd purchased for her when he'd bought the sex toys. It would cover her from the bottom of her breasts to the flare of her ass, leaving all the erogenous parts exposed for him to sample.

"You call this dressing for dinner," she said with a giggle when he cinched her into the garment.

"Uh huh," he said, cupping her breasts as they billowed out of the top, rubbing her nipples, making her squirm.

She moaned and leaned toward him. "More."

He shook his head and dropped his hands. "Wait for it." When she glared at him, he smiled. "Bend over the bed, Honor," he said, pulling her lube and butt plug out of the drawer.

He watched her eyes widen when she saw them in his hands, still she bent over obediently, her lush tits pillowed against the mattress.

"So you're still going to tease me with them," she grumbled.

He stroked the lush globes of her ass, his cock throbbing when she pressed back at him, knowing she was trying to force the issue.

"You're not the only one who's being teased," he said, caressing her already creamy sex, his lubed finger tickling her puckered anus. "I'm not going to take you until you're ready for me," he said.

She let out a moan when he slipped his finger into her heat, her body rippling on him, and he stifled an aching to take her. Instead, he lubed the butt plug and slipped it into her feeling her shudder.

"Up now," he said, helping her to stand. She let out a helpless whimper and turned a sultry gaze on him.

"I seem to be the only one that's dressed master," she said in a sassy tone.

"I'll be wearing you," he replied with a smile when she blushed. It was a delight that he could still shock her. He flicked on his Ipod and sultry jazz floated through the air. "A little mood music."

"I'm surprised it's not Arabic music."

"I have eclectic tastes."

"So I noticed."

He walked over to the table and pulled out her chair. "Madame."

Blushing, she walked over and let him seat her, gasping when her bottom hit the seat. "You'll pay for this," she muttered, glaring up at him.

"Hold that thought." He chuckled as he went into the kitchen to serve the Moroccan stew. When he placed a platter before her, she took a deep whiff, her tummy grumbling.

"This smells wonderful," she said, beaming up at him.

"Thanks. It's an old family recipe, but I've added a few new touches of my own," he said pleased.

"You cooked this?" she said in surprise.

"When you live like I do, you learn to cook or settle for eating out of tin cans," he said going to get the pita bread. He took a seat pleased to note that she'd waited for him to sit down before she ate. "Enjoy," he said, dipping his spoon into his bowl enjoying the savory and spicy flavors bursting on his tongue. He gazed at Honor hungry for more than just food.

Her lovely face, her sexy tits tumbling out of the bustier, the strawberry pink nipples semi-hard. He knew that with one touch from him they'd turn to hard little jewels. She made his mouth water.

"Spicy," she said, taking a bite.

"Not too hot," he said, watching her.

"No. I like it hot," she said, and blushed at the double entendre.

"I noticed." Knowing he should let her eat, he concentrated on his own food, tearing a pita and dipping it into the sauce. "The meal is like me, a blending of two different, and some would say, contrary cultures."

"Tell me about it."

"My mother's Greek, my father's from Jordan, they defied their families and married."

"Like Romeo and Juliet."

"Kind of, it was even more complicated because their fathers were business rivals."

"Ah, two different crime syndicates."

His mouth twitched. "Some people would call them that. They prefer to think of themselves as businessmen."

"Sorry," she said, blushing. "I didn't mean to sound so judgmental."

"It's okay, they were sharks, and both drove a hard bargain."

"Well, I take it that it all worked out."

"My parents were able to get them to work together, bury the hatchet so to speak. And they're still happily married. So yes, I'd say it worked. I'm the oldest of three children. My dad managed to keep harmony in the family through the family trade."

"That's nice."

"In my family, it works. The fact that I still have to work to keep everyone happy is a role I happily take on. Tell me about your family."

"Not that much to tell. I'm an only child," she said.

"Your parents didn't believe in big families?"

"It wasn't so much that as that my dad was in trouble with the law, as well as being a total workaholic." She looked at him and blushed. "Don't get me wrong in many ways it was an ideal childhood growing up in a cute little tourist town, getting all of my parents love."

He smiled realizing that he was somewhat like her workaholic father, his mind usually on the business. Crown Jewelers didn't run itself, and he was deeply involved with the day-to-day affairs. He realized that someday he'd have to cede some of the control, learn to delegate, but he wasn't ready to let go yet.

His one getaway being this two-week vacation he took to the villa. That's why this idyll with Honor was so special. But he also knew that when playtime was over he'd have to get back to his usual routine. When Honor had cleaned her bowl, he stood reaching for her dishes.

"Let me help," she said, starting to stand.

"You're my guest," he said, waving her back down into her seat. She settled back with a pleased smile.

"Time for dessert," he said, seeing her blush. She remembered his statement that he'd have her for dessert. He came back with bowls of plump strawberries, dates, chocolate, and honey. Then he sat down and reached out to pull her onto his lap, drinking in her needy gasp. "Hungry?" he asked, feeding her a date dipped in honey.

"Yes, I'm famished." She nibbled the tidbit from his hand.

"What are you thinking," he said, his cock stirring as she licked honey off his fingers with sexy little flicks of her pink tongue. He could still picture it swirling around his cock.

"That this is crazy. That I don't do things like this."

"You do now," he said, dipping a strawberry in the hot melted chocolate and feeding it to her. His heart melted when she shyly nibbled the confection out of his fingers and then licked his fingers. "Feed me," he said leaning back.

She smiled and picked up a strawberry, dipping it first in honey and then chocolate.

His body stiffened even more when she brought the fruit to his mouth and he ate it off her fingers, tasting her as well as the confection. His cock was burning, throbbing under her lush ass. He dipped his finger in the honey bowl and then painted her sexy lips with the sticky sweet.

She was breathing hard, her tits jiggling a little, her lips parted. She whimpered, leaning closer and he kissed her, his tongue mastering hers just as surely as he ached to master her. She kissed him back, whimpering when he slicked honey over her nipples and then broke the kiss to lick it off. He sucked her nipples and then his teeth closed over it, scraping it gently as he tugged. She let out a squeal, wiggling her ass on him, making him crazy. When he swept the bowls aside and laid her on the table aching to taste her she was sobbing.

She spread her legs for him crying out, "Oh yes. Taste me there."

He flashed her a wicked smile, bending to do just that, coating her creamy pink sex with honey and then leaning forward to leisurely lick it off, with long slow strokes of his tongue.

She cried out arching toward him, and he held her hips still seeing how she reacted to the restraint. She gasped, shuddering, her pussy quivering. He growled and sucked her clit into his mouth, drawing hard on it.

She shrieked, on the edge of coming, and he let her go. Honor shuddered, swearing. It pleased him that she was so hot for him.

"I need to..."

"You can't come yet," he said as she glared up at him. He cast a hot glance over her abandoned pose, her nipples like hard berries, and her glistening sex open for him, her ass quivering around the butt plug. With a possessive tug, he swept her into his arms and carried her to the bed laying her in the middle.

Then he reached for a silk scarf saying, "Give me your hand, Honor." He waited breathlessly wondering if she'd obey and give herself over to him completely. When she smiled and held out her hand, he let out the breath he'd been holding.

He tied it loosely to the bedpost making her gasp and then quickly walked around the bed to secure her other wrist. She trembled when he gazed down at her.

"So I'm your prisoner of love," she said with a smile.

He nodded, his cock throbbing, and then bent to kiss her, his hand squeezing her breast then rolling her nipple. She started to arch off the mattress. He pulled away to smile at her. "Lay still, if you want me to make you come."

"Control freak," she muttered going still.

"That's better." He wanted to make her ache for him like he ached for her. He stripped his clothes feeling her fascinated gaze follow him as he walked over to the dresser and pulled out a vibrator. She took one look at it and gasped, making him smile. "We're going to put your cock versus vibrator theory to the test," he said walking to the bed.

"Oh my," she said with a grin.

He got into bed with her, his hand slicking down her body to caress her hot curves, toying with her nipples, smoothing over the bustier to cup her mound. He buzzed her left nipple, smiling when she cried out, then withdrew it asking, "Tell me, concubine. Who do you belong to?"

She arched against the bed shuddering. "You," she moaned.

He smiled, buzzing one nipple again and then bending to suck the other into his mouth, drawing on it until she was mewling, and when her legs thrashed he threw his thigh over them pinning her down.

"Take me now," she demanded. "I can't wait."

"Yes you can," he said, buzzing the vibrator against her mound, just grazing her clit. She cried out, quivering, and he drank in the intoxicating sound. Only he could make her feel this way.

His damned cock bucked against her thigh killing him but he wanted to last just a little longer. He spread her legs a little and played the vibrator over the folds of her blushing pink sex, watching it ripple against the device. Then he stroked the vibrators tip over the stretched little ring of her asshole, and she whimpered.

He damned near came rubbing his hot cock against her silky thigh. "Which do you want filling your hungry pussy?" he asked, watching her.

She pressed her leg against him, crying out, "Either, both, I don't know," she wailed. "Just put me out of my misery."

He smiled at her candid answer and slipped the cock ring over his swollen member wanting to give her all she needed. Knowing he could stand it no more, he settled between her legs.

"Open your eyes and look at me when I take you," he demanded, and her eyes swept open. The passion glazed look in them almost made him come. Instead, he let the head of his cock press against her cunt. "It's going to be a tight fit because of the butt plug and the cock ring. If it's too much, tell me."

She growled and arched up trying to capture him.

He let out a chuckle and switched on the cock rings vibrator, realizing she was just as far gone. The vibration was almost painful to his aching cock and when he pressed it against her, she cried out in wonder.

"Don't tell me they make them to fit over your..."

"It's called a cock ring," he said, growling when he eased into her creamy cunt, feeling her tense at the invasion. Then she rippled around him moaning and he thrust the rest of the way in, the pressure almost making him come.

He started moving in and out of her until she was gasping, her sugar walls clenching, milking at his driving cock. She was almost there, he knew but they had to come together. "Come now," he demanded grinding against her.

She cried out convulsing around him. "Oh my god, Alex."

He shuddered, her orgasm pushing him over the edge, making him explode as he spilled his load against her cervix. "Honor," he gritted out.

Chapter Eleven

I put away the lunch dishes in Alex's kitchen and walked back out to the main room to find him sitting at the table typing into a laptop computer. My jaw literally dropped when I looked at the unexpected sight.

Somehow, I never associated the oh-so-earthy sheik, who'd introduced me to bondage and cock rings last night, with the computer age. He was wearing board shorts again his feet and chest bare while I was still naked. At least some things never changed, I thought with a rueful smile. "You're on the web," I said shocked.

He looked up at me and smiled at my startled reaction. "Of course. I'm not all that primitive, love. Come and look," he said, beckoning me forward.

I walked around the table to see what he was doing, my hungry gaze raking over him. I tore my gaze away to look at the computer screen. The photos we'd taken yesterday were on the screen, including the nudes. I really wanted the one of him but knew we couldn't take it to a photo shop.

"They're wonderful," I said. "Especially the ones you took," I said, realizing he had a talent.

"Thanks." He pressed a button to print them out and stood to walk over to the photo printer.

I gazed at the high tech equipment, impressed. "You're really into photography, aren't you?"

"It's a passion," he said, smiling at me.

I could see other folders in his pictures file on the laptop screen. I itched to see what else he'd photographed. "Do you mind if I look?"

"Feel free," he said, stacking the photos he'd just printed.

I opened the file and gasped when I saw the folder was filled with photos of beautiful jewelry. Of course, he'd photograph another passion. I cast a look over at him, wondering if I could break him of it, and then sighed. He was what he was, and I couldn't change him.

Now I understood why my mother had turned a blind eye to my father's indiscretions. I looked back down at the photographs of the jewels; they were actually as exquisite as the jewels themselves, looking professionally done. That was my only chance, I knew, the slim chance that I could convince him to throw off his family obligations and go into photography as a living.

"Do you like them?" he asked, walking back over to me.

I nodded. "You did a masterful job capturing the jewel's brilliance."

"Jewelry's another passion of mine," he said, smirking.

"I noticed," I said, a little sadly. If he thought this was funny, he was dead wrong.

"Which one is your favorite?" he asked, watching me closely.

I gazed at the thumbnail clips on the screen realizing that my answer was for some reason important to him. The collection of jewels were all different and all exquisite. "They're beautiful, but they're not for me."

"Why not?" He frowned and clicked a key on the laptop to bring the photos into full size and have them play in a slide show.

It seemed like I'd hurt his feelings, which was crazy seeing they were stolen goods. "Don't get me wrong, they're beautiful. However, if I ever made enough to afford a luxury like this, I'd choose something plainer, yet more unique." Besides, I wasn't letting him give me any of his ill-gotten goods. I glanced at him to see if my answer had mollified him and found him scowling. I had hurt his feelings.

"You think they're too gaudy?" he said, tight lipped.

So, that's what had his back up. He thought I was saying that he had bad taste. Nothing could be further from the truth. "No. They're beautiful; works of art even, but too rich for me. Like I said, I'd design something a little bit different."

"Like what, for instance?" he asked, his brow arched.

Oh boy, I just kept sinking in deeper. "It's kind of hard to describe," I said, hoping to change the subject.

"Try," he insisted, then thrust a piece of paper my way. "Better yet, show me."

Why was he being so persistent about this? I had no desire to ruin what was our last day together by arguing. I sighed and picked up a pencil deciding to humor him. I sketched the design in my head. A strand of simulated pearls, with a heart shaped simulated ruby as a pendant.

"How's this?" I watched his indulgent smile turn to surprise as he gazed at the pendant.

"You're really good."

"It's a hobby," I said, mimicking his words about photography.

"Some hobby. How'd you know about the alligator clip?"

"You caught me. I used to make jewelry for my mother's gift shop. It was more unique than the mass-produced junk she'd bought from China and it sold better. I learned to bead from my Native American girlfriends. I'd probably still be at it if my mother hadn't pushed me out of the nest and encouraged me to follow my dream."

"I'm stunned. It's like you were made for me," he said, pulling me into his arms.

"Nice." I snuggled against him, feeling close to him when our love affair was at its end. Tomorrow I'd hop the ferry, without the necklace, and go home. I wouldn't collect twenty grand, I couldn't betray Alex, I loved him. I knew it to be true even as I thought it, but I also knew that I'd never tell him. I was a diversion to him, nothing more. I decided not to dwell on tomorrow and concentrate on making the most of our last day and night together. I was still a little shocked that he'd turned me into a wanton woman, but I couldn't deny I liked it. I went on tiptoes to kiss him, and drawing back saw a startled look on his face.

"What was that for?"

"Making this a vacation to remember," I said with a smile.

"For me, too," he said, rising to his feet.

"Wait until I get back home," I said thinking about sharing the news with Sheri. His eyes narrowed as he gazed down at me.

"Just what are your plans?"

His hostile question caught me by surprise. Was it possible that he was jealous? The thought made me glow inside. "I just thought of someone I could share the news with."

"Hal?" he said, in a clipped tone.

"No." Let him worry. It was the same thing I'd been going through picturing him with the countess and countless others.

He reached out to switch off the computer and then took my arm urging me out the door. "Time for our swim."

"Isn't it a bit early?" I asked, glancing at the clock as we walked out the door.

"I'm expecting company tonight so we'll have to adjust our schedule."

His words shocked me. I didn't want to share him and I was naked. I scowled at him and saw him grinning.

"Don't worry, love, I'll give you something to wear."

"I'll bet," I said, rolling my eyes. "How about giving me back my passport."

"If you like." He picked me up and carried me into the surf.

I was shocked at his seeming capitulation and stared up at his amused expression as he carried me into deeper water. It felt as if my whole world had brightened. He was beginning to trust me.

Grinning, he dove down dunking us both. I came up sputtering. I took one look at his twinkling eyes and let out a laugh, enjoying his playful side. He captured me in his arms.

"You're my prisoner."

"Don't you mean concubine?" I said, smiling up at him.

"That too," he agreed.

My body heated as I pressed against him. And he surged into me with a groan, taking me slow and deep. I

99

was already there and I cried out as my body tightened around him. His hold on me tightened as he followed me over the edge, holding me as if he never wanted to let me go.

"About our hobbies," he said.

I glanced up at him and smiled. "What about them?"

"Would you be happy if they came to pass?"

"You just keep astounding me," I said.

"That's good," he said, carrying me back through the surf. He walked back to the blanket he'd spread on the beach, and laid down pulling me atop him.

I lifted my head to smile at him. "You've really been thinking about making some changes?"

"Uh huh," he said, watching me. "Do you think that I can?"

"I have complete faith in you." I kissed him, thrilled he was seeing things my way. Maybe there was hope for us yet. I knew I was rapidly building a fantasy happy ever after ending for us in my mind but I couldn't help it. Besides, it distracted me from wondering about the company coming.

Chapter Twelve

That evening, Alex dressed in linen trousers and a silk shirt, sliding loafers onto his feet. Only the imminent arrival of his cousins would have made him get dressed. He was well aware that Honor, naked by the bed, watched his every move.

She was a little nervous about the company but he'd promised he'd dress her and he would, just not the way she probably imagined.

He pulled the pink and mint green colored harem costume he'd brought out of the closet and laid it on the bed. "Come here," he said, crooking his finger.

He studied her astounded reaction as she gazed at the harem costume. Would she go for it? All he had to do was keep her distracted for the night, and then he could think about keeping her. Her eyes twinkled and her mouth curved in a slow grin.

"This is what you meant by dressing for dinner," she said, smiling.

"That's right," he said, relaxing.

"And when do the other harem girls show up?" she teased.

His warm gaze raked over her. "Love, you're the only harem girl I want." He watched her blush prettily and then picked up her tote bag from the dresser. She hadn't even noticed it. "Your bag."

Her eyes lit up as she took the bag. "You kept your promise."

"I always do," he said. It was a good thing he'd ordered the costume along with the sex toys because he didn't want to give her back her clothes just yet. He just had to hold her to him a little longer. And the idea of her naked in front of his lecherous cousins made him jealous. As it was, he knew they'd enjoy riling him up, and probably make passes at her.

He crooked his finger at her and she obediently walked toward him, setting her bag down on the bed. He smiled at her sweet compliance, his cock throbbing.

Trying to stifle his need, he picked up the pantalets, handed them to Honor, and watched her slip into the bottoms. They fit her like a glove, riding low on her hips below her navel, a double layer of embroidered fabric covering her sex, and then the legs puffed out in see through fabric the cuffed at the ankles.

He smiled and pressed a round cut emerald into her navel making her gasp. He stood back to admire the affect, and then watched her shimmy into the 'barely there' top. The neckline cut low to expose her cleavage ended right below her breasts, leaving her midriff bare.

His body ached with repressed need as he gazed at her. He had a sudden premonition that his brilliant plan just might back fire on him. Then he gave her matching slippers to put on and pinned a silk veil over her golden curls.

Finally, he pulled the emerald necklace out of his shaving kit and fastened it around her neck. She looked like a vision, like an Arabian princess.

"What do you think?" he said, taking her shoulders and turning her to face the mirror.

"My goodness, I look like I just stepped out of a mirage," she said, her eyes twinkling.

He smiled. "A very sexy mirage."

"What do you think?" she asked.

"That you look way too sexy to show to my cousins," he answered, wondering if he should bundle her up and hide her. They were going to give her the stupid loyalty test; he just knew it, even though he'd forbidden it.

"Thanks." She gazed at her reflection in the mirror. "I feel like I've fallen into an Arabian nights fantasy dream."

"Complete with your own sheik to play with."

"That's the best part," she said, gazing at his reflection in the mirror.

He smiled at her admission. She did care about him, but was it really enough for her to abandon her plans? Footsteps outside alerted him his guests were here. Alex took her hand and led her toward the door. "Come on. We've got company."

He opened the door letting in Nick and Karim bristling when both men looked around him to eye Honor. He gave them both a repressive glare that usually worked and this time didn't. They continued to gaze at her with amusement and frank masculine approval. He couldn't help feeling jealous.

"Honor, come meet my guests," Alex said, watching her as she stepped forward, a pretty blush covering her face. He knew her reaction would be like catnip to his tomcat younger cousins.

"Hello," she said shyly.

"You've already met Nick," Alex said, patting his Greek cousin on the shoulder.

"Nice to see you again," she said, frowning at him.

Alex grinned at her feisty reaction. She definitely recalled that he'd offered to arrest her.

"Not half as nice as it is to see you again, my lovely," Nick said smoothly, his eyes twinkling as he stared at her.

She let out a little gasp when he brushed a soft kiss against her palm.

"Stop trying to steal my girl," Alex said to break them up and loved the startled smile Honor gave him. She was his girl, and he'd find a way to keep her.

Nick smirked and nodded, sauntering into the house. Alex knew he was acting like a jealous fool but he couldn't help it. Then Karim stepped up his amused glance lingering on Alex's face.

"And this is Karim," Alex said.

"Charmed," Karim said, leaning forward to kiss Honor.

She frowned and ducked his peck so that it landed on her cheek.

"You're fast," Karim said with a laugh.

"And you're naughty," she shot back at him.

Alex watched the byplay with approval and came up to loop a possessive arm around her. "Pour us some drinks, Honor, while we get down to business."

She nodded and hurried into the kitchen.

Alex watched her go and then turned to give his laughing cousins a warning glare. "Cut the crap, I don't want a friggen loyalty test," he ordered, fuming when they just laughed. He should have known they'd ignore him even though he was president of the company.

They both took time off from their regular lives and worked as couriers for Crown Jewels when he needed them.

"Come on," he said, leading the way to the poker table. "I'll want you two to make a special run and take the goods into the city for me tomorrow," he said, and the crash of a glass in the kitchen made him look up. Had Honor overheard?

She blushed and looked away. "Oops, I dropped a glass."

"Did you cut yourself?" he said, alarmed by her sudden pallor.

"I'm fine," she said with a half smile. "Go back to your card game. I just want to sweep this up."

"Be careful," he said and looked back at his cousins. They were both grinning at him. Well hell, next thing he knew they'd have the village matchmaker on his ass.

Nick smiled. "Don't tell me you're actually going to get a life, stay on vacation with her."

"Yeah, I think I am," he said, keeping a wary eye on Honor as she swept the broken glass off the floor. He could have sworn she was upset but she seemed fine now. "You can tell my secretary that I'm otherwise occupied," he said.

"We noticed," Karim said, casting a burning look Honor's way. "The harem girl get up is a nice touch."

"Don't get any ideas," Alex said, picturing his wealthy cousin carrying Honor off to his harem.

The fact that Karim was independently wealthy, yet got a kick out of working for him on occasion, said he didn't care much about moral conventions.

But he knew his cousin would never poach from him, the four of them had a bond.

Karim chuckled. "Don't worry, with Angelica my nights are currently full."

Alex remembered the little gold digger his cousin referred to. She'd failed the brother's loyalty test but Karim had kept her anyway because she amused him. But lately, he'd seen the signs that things were coming apart. He nodded and turned to Nick just as Honor started walking their way. "Don't forget to say your piece."

"Oh, by the way, Alex, the ferry's not running," Jose said loudly as Honor reached them.

Alex tried not to roll his eyes at the bad acting and then turned to glance at Honor to see if she bought it. Her wry grin was mysterious but he couldn't help noticing the long lingering look she gave him. What was that all about? She smiled and set the tray on the table passing out glasses of Ouzo.

"Your snacks, my master," she said playfully as she handed his last.

Alex smiled, relaxing, realizing she was playing her concubine roll to the hilt. And why not, it was her fantasy. Then Jose smiled, looping his arm around her waist, drawing her to him, and she let out a gasp of excitement, her face flushing.

Recognizing the excited look on her face, Alex frowned. He glowered as Jose playfully spanked her sexy fanny watching Honor's glowing face. Damn it all, she was responding.

"Don't be so greedy, adelphos," Karim said to Jose, grabbing Honor's wrist and tugging her away from his cousin.

Karim pulled her onto his lap, his hand flattening on her bare midriff and he shot Alex a challenging glance.

Alex's hand clenched as he met his cousin's look, interpreting it as, you'd better fight for her or risk losing her to another man. Hell, he'd already figured that out for himself. He stiffened, growling when Karim smiled and bent to kiss Honor. She gasped and turned her head avoiding his kiss, and Alex smiled finally able to breathe again. She didn't want anyone else.

"Stop teasing her, adelphos," Alex said, and grabbed her arm, pulling Honor onto his lap. She went with a purr melting against him, making his cock throb.

His hand cupped her breast and she hid her head on his shoulder trembling against him. Her needy response made him crazy and he stroked her nipple feeling it bud as she stifled a whimper.

"You're welcome," Karim said, rising.

"We'll be back at zero ten hundred for the ice," Nick said, following him out.

Alex held Honor, his heart lightening as he bent to kiss her. She hadn't freaked out about having to stay here because the ferry wasn't running. And, shockingly, she'd passed his loyalty test with flying colors. Everything was going to work out. After Nick and Karim left with the shipment, he'd come clean with Honor. He was keeping her.

Chapter Thirteen

I moaned as Alex stroked my tingling nipple through the harem girl costume and dimly heard the door close behind his gang. I was more turned on than I'd ever been and my heart was breaking.

Alex was incorrigible; I should have realized that from the beginning. A man who headed a crime family couldn't go straight. I could even forgive that, but I couldn't forgive his trying to con me and hold me trapped.

I'd just have to save him from himself and make a clean break of things. But first, I wanted one more night in his arms. The heat of his palm made my nipple bud and tingle, and I arched against it, whimpering.

I broke the kiss; scattering kisses down his neck, his delighted laugh spurring me on. Then I wiggled off his lap, making him groan in complaint and try to grab me, but I jumped out of range. I wanted to give him a memory of me he'd never forget.

Smiling, I flicked on his Ipod and started belly dancing to the sultry jazz, trying to tempt him, wiggling my hips as he sat up and took notice. His eyes turned sultry as he watched me. I shook my breasts and then turned my back on him, undoing the front closure on my top. Then I playfully slipped it off my shoulder and turned to look at him. He was breathing hard. Good. I slipped the top off, and cupping my breasts turned and smiled. I held them out, stepped closer, leaning forward to brush my hard nipples against his mouth. He flicked out his tongue licking them, making me shiver, and tried to grab me. I jumped back and he swore.

"Tease."

"I learned from the master," I said.

Then I started to peel down my harem pants and he went still. I turned my back on him bending over a little to tempt him as I peeled them down. He began to sweat. Excellent. I stepped out of my pantaloons, and walked toward him, taking off my headscarf remembering how he'd tied me to the bedposts with them.

I had something a little simpler in mind. I unbuttoned his shirt, running my hands over his chest teasing his nipples, and making him swear once again. Then I smiled and opened his pants. His cock popped out and I leaned in to cup it in my hands, stroking him.

I smiled, swirling the silky scarf over his cock. He hissed, bucking. Excellent. I looped it around his cock and balls tightening it a bit, then licked the head. He arched and started to rise.

"Stay put or I'll stop," I warned, feeling my power. He glared at me and sat back down. I smiled while tightening the scarf a little more, and then took him into my greedy mouth. I sucked hard, feeling his body tighten, and took him as deep as I could.

Choking and backing off a little to take him deep again. Feeling him buck, I tightened the scarf and sucked harder, he came spurting into my mouth, and I drank him down, draining him. When it was over, I sat back on my heels and gazed up at him.

"Little witch," he said with a smile.

"You made me one," I said, my body aglow. All I wanted to do was concentrate on the sensations my sheik caused in me. My sex was quivering as I knelt there, my nipples hard as jewels. He reached out to cup one and I shivered, moaning, making him smile.

"On your feet, slave girl. It's time for your paddling," he said.

A delighted shiver shot through me. He was actually going to use that tantalizing black paddle I'd seen on the shelf. He stood and pulled me to my feet and into his arms.

I went with an excited shiver knowing this was only the beginning. I gasped when he carried me into the shower instead of taking me to bed, my body throbbing for him. Quivering with anticipation, I rose to my feet and he reached out to grab my arm when I wobbled, steadying me. I moaned, burning from the contact, and leaned into him. A little fission of excitement and alarm zinged through me

"Bend over the back of the chair," he said with a growl.

I nodded, my body clinging to him, feeling bemused when he spun me around and had me bend over and rest my hands on the teak bench. I moaned as he stroked me, playing with my clit, pussy, and the sensitive flesh around my anus. Then he slicked cool lube on my ass and I shuddered. His cock throbbed nice and hot as it brushed against me, promising passion.

Blushing, I did as he said, bending over the padded back with a gasp. I moaned, my body quivering as I watched him walk over to the dresser and pick up the paddle. If a hand spanking, made me crazy what would a paddling do? I'd probably be begging him to fuck me by the time it was through. He smiled and stood beside me, his hand slicking down my flanks, and then he pulled back the paddle and gave my left cheek a rapid smack, making me gasp at the stinging heat.

"I think you like this," he said with a chuckle.

I moaned in embarrassment, knowing it was true, as he continued to paddle me, flooding my body with heat. My sex and bottom were spasming, and a cream of arousal made me wet. I arched back at him leaning into the teasing, stoked on fire.

"You're mine," he said with a final smack.

"I'm yours." I sighed when he dropped the paddle and caressed my hot bottom with his big hands, his stiff cock brushing against my hip. I was pulsing, almost there, I needed to come.

"You're ass is so hot," he said, rubbing me.

I laughed, amused at the double entendre. "Because of you," I said, moaning when his cock brushed against my hot bottom, and my ass quivered.

"Do you still want me to take your ass?" he asked.

"Oh yes," I said, throbbing with need. If he denied me, I'd have to take matters into my own hands, maybe handcuff him to the bed and have my way with him. Then I saw him pick up the lube and smiled. He wasn't teasing.

I bit back a gasp when he slicked the cool lube over my quivering anus, slowly stroking me until I arched out at his teasing finger. Then he withdrew, making me gasp with disappointment, only to step up behind me.

I moaned when I felt the broad head of his magnificent cock press against me. This was it. I was really going to get it.

When he pressed firmly against me, just the tip of his cock entering my quivering opening, I cried out at the invasion. He was bigger than the butt plug he'd made me use but I wanted this. He froze, bending to kiss my nape.

"You okay, Honor?"

"Yes," I said, more breathlessly than I would have like as my ass rippled on the head of his cock. I felt stretched her open, completely taken, as he leaned over me enveloping me in his heat.

"Take me now, damn it, or I'll lose my mind," I demand surging back at him fearing he'd stop. He gripped my hips firmly to stop me and I grumbled.

116

He laughed at my fiercely worded order, the blunt head of his cock pressing insistently against me. "We do this my way," he said.

I panted when he eased inside me, inch by tantalizing inch, my legs trembling, only his grip on my hips holding me up until I took him all.

He rested there, letting me get used to the invasion, as a heat wave washed through me, no doubt staining me from face to ass. I couldn't help it, feeling totally claimed by him.

I moaned helplessly as my ass rippled, milking his cock at the same time that my sex quivered. I let out a breath, gasping when my body rippled on him. "Yes. I think so. It feels so dirty, kind of good and bad."

"Honey, we've just begun," he said, gently pulling part way out to rock back inside me.

I quivered, relaxing around his surging cock, turned on beyond belief and arched back to meet his thrusts.

"Slowly, love," he said, pulling out to slip back inside.

Heat surged through me when he did it again, building a driving rhythm that made me cry out. I rocked back against him, his balls slapping into me. I cried out

117

when he rocked into me, setting off tidal waves of quivers through my pussy and ass. It was even better than I'd imagined, and twice as naughty. I let out a breathy cry of pleasure.

Then he reached for my clit, making me scream. He toyed with it while he stroked me harder, his cock throbbing inside me, driving me over the edge.

"That's it, come for me, Honor," he husked.

I did, crying out as I convulsed, my ass milking his cock as I came, screaming his name.

He thrust into me once more groaning, shooting his cum inside me, just as my world went hazy. When I came to I was cuddled in his arms and he looked down at me, worriedly.

"Never scare me like that again," he demanded.

I just smiled sadly up at him trying to memorize his face. He'd never get the chance to make me swoon again. I was going to save him from himself.

Just as the sun was rising, I rolled away from Alex, knowing that I had to leave before I weakened and changed my mind. I was scarily close to making the stupid mistake. Alex was finally sleeping deeply after our marathon love making session. I eased away from his heat, and quietly slipped out of bed.

Having no idea where he'd hidden the clothes I'd come here with, I slipped back into the harem girl costume. Had it only been four short days ago that I'd come here on my insane mission to steal back the necklace? It seemed like a lifetime ago. So much had changed.

I lingered, gazing at my sexy sheik knowing I had to run, I had to save him from disaster. I clasped the necklace around my neck.

Alex was going to be pissed to lose it, and it went against my old personal code, but I had no choice but to steal the necklace back from him. But first, I had to make sure he wouldn't follow me.

I pulled the rusty old handcuffs my dad had foisted on me when I'd moved to the big city, out of my tote bag. At least I hadn't had to use his homemade mace on Alex. Who knew what kind of damage that stuff could do.

I tiptoed over to the head of the bed and gently clicked one side over Alex's right wrist wincing at the loud noise in the quiet room. Alex snored and I relaxed. I was going to get away clean. I quickly secured the other side of the handcuffs to the wrought iron bedpost. Then I walked over and set the key on the dresser next to the paddle he'd used on me. Nick and Karim would be here at ten. They could release him.

I gave him one last look, and hurried to the door before I could weaken and change my mind. Shutting the door behind me, I made for the pier, running across the beach. Within moments, I'd cast off from the moorings and let the dinghy drift a ways out before starting the engine, and speeding out to sea in the general direction of the mainland.

Chapter Fourteen

Alex woke the next morning, his head a little muzzy, his body stiff, when he heard a buzzing sound. He'd been dreaming about buzzing engines. He tried to move and swore when he realized he couldn't. Something held him fast.

He looked at the handcuff locking him to the bedpost, recognizing it in an instant, and relaxed. Any moment now, Honor would come slinking into the room and ravage him. Then he spotted her tote bag missing from the top of the dresser and swore.

Shit, she'd run out on him again, and just when he'd thought he could trust her. When he caught her, he'd paddle her ass until she couldn't sit down, and then he'd fuck her until she never even thought about running again. Her sweet smell still clung to the bed, and he groaned, his cock rousing.

How had she even had the will, much less the energy to escape after their nightlong lovemaking session? He'd turned to her time and again, introducing her to every kinky technique he knew and even making up a few and she'd been insatiable, urging him on.

And that's when it hit him, she'd planned to leave and that's why she'd teased him so last night, on fire for him. He cursed himself knowing he was to blame. He should have heeded Karim's advice and locked a precious jewel like Honor in his own private harem. He struggled against the bonds of the old handcuffs but it held, damn it all. Then he sighed knowing how bad he'd miscalculated. He should have trusted her with the truth. Karim and Nick would be here at ten, but would he be able to catch her?

What seemed like an eternity later, Nick and Karim walked through the door.

He glared at them, taking in their startled expressions as they stared back at him. "You're late."

Nick tipped back his head and roared with laughter. "Things get out of hand after we left?"

"What do you think," Alex muttered, glaring back at him.

"I told you to lock her in a harem," Karim said, his lips twitching.

"I'm thinking about it," Alex said. "Is my launch gone?"

Nick glanced out the door and nodded. "It sure is."

"Shit," Alex said, picturing her out alone in his tiny launch. Damn it all, why had she taken such a risk? Because he hadn't offered her any alternative, he told himself bitterly. This was all his fucking fault.

"She's on her way to Michael," he said, praying that she'd actually get there in one piece.

"Oh man," Jose said sympathetically.

Karim picked up the key from the dresser, his brow arching when he spied the paddle. "Cheer up pal, at least she didn't leave you stranded."

"Unlock me then, and get me some pants," Alex said already plotting the best way to get her back. The only thing he knew was that he had to get her back.

Chapter Fifteen

My heart lifted when I sped into the little seaport where I'd originally taken the ferry. I smiled taking it as a good omen. I must have a wild guardian angel looking after me to lead me here.

It'd been a bit of a rocky trip but I'd made it knowing I owed my good fortune having grown up on a lake. Leaving Alex had been the hardest thing I'd ever done, but it was for his own good. I knew if he had called out to me, I'd probably still be with him.

I wished I could have taken the time to leave a note, but what was there to say? That I loved him, I thought blinking back the tears misting my eyes. It was true but I knew that he didn't love me back.

I cruised past the ferry's jetty looking for a place to ditch Alex's dinghy and got lucky when I sighted a public boat dock. I pulled up, tying off, and leaped out of the dinghy tote bag in hand. I wanted to get this heartbreaking business over with fast. I had to get to the lawyer's office in a fancy high rise building in the center of town.

My soft slippers with the funny upturned toes made a slapping noise as I walked along the pier, and I felt ultra conspicuous. The local fishermen stopped what they were doing to stare and whistle at me, a few throwing out earthy compliments that made me blush. They probably thought I was some kind of hooker just like Alex had claimed to when we first met.

I knew then and there that trotting through Athens in my get up wasn't an option. My ass would be bruised from all the pinches I'd receive, and I'd probably risk getting arrested for public indecency. I'd just have to bite the bullet and spend what was left of my cash on a taxi. At least I still had my plane ticket to get back home.

Raising my chin defiantly and glaring back at the hooting idiots, I stomped toward the end of the dock and managed to wave down a taxi who'd just dropped off a fare. The driver gave me a doubtful look when I jumped into his cab, but then I rattled off the address I wanted, pulling cash out of my bag, and he took off.

Thrown back against the seat as he accelerated I coached myself for the scene to come. First, I'd tackle the countess's attorney in his office. At least I wasn't likely to encounter the other woman. I'd turn the necklace over to him and tell him in no uncertain terms what the stupid countess could do with her blood money.

There was no way I'd turn Alex in. Then I'd be on my way. I'd high tail it back to my hotel, pick up my things, and catch the evening flight home. I could do this.

When the taxi pulled up at the sleek glass and steel high-rise office building, I sighed. Taking the last step to walk away from Alex, and all the delights he offered, was going to be painful. But there was no sense in putting it off; I was nothing but a vacation fling to him.

I paid the cab driver and got out of the cab blushing when people on the street stopped to stare at me in my harem girl costume. The green stone even still glittered in my navel. I walked past the curious bystanders and entered the building. Why not, I was a curiosity. I held my head high, rushed into the elevator, and punched the button for the penthouse.

Once I reached the top floor, I stalked down the long hall to the lawyer's unmarked door, again thinking it odd that he didn't have his name on it, instead it said CJ Ltd. I entered, startling his secretary, an older woman who was on the phone; she swept my get-up with an amused glance. Considering the kind of clients he dealt with, she'd probably seen everything.

"Please hold," she said, punching a button on the phone. She looked up at Honor and smiled. "Michael's on the phone," she said. "If you'll have a seat I'll tell him you're here. I know he wants to see you."

Some of my fury evaporated when I was told to wait. When the older lady gazed pointedly at a chair, I subsided into it. I had time until my flight, and this couldn't be put off.

She pushed a button on the console and then turned to smile at me. "Would you like some tea, my dear?"

"No, thank you," I said, folding my hands on my lap. This little diversion would be funny if it wasn't breaking my heart.

Then a light blinked on her console and she said. "You can go in now."

I stood up with as much dignity as I could muster and walked toward the lawyer's office opening his door. He sat behind his cluttered desk, his dark eyes sweeping over my scantily clad form. He was tall, with the same coloring as Alex. Realizing it made my heart pang. Still, he was nowhere near as handsome as my sheik and he did nothing for me.

"Come in," he said waving me toward a chair.

I ignored his gesture to sit and stepped up to his desk. I wouldn't be here that long. I noticed his eyes were twinkling with amusement as he looked at me. Was he laughing at me? I glared back at him.

"I see that you've come with the necklace," he said, his gaze lingering on the necklace I wore. "That wasn't part of our new deal. He should have told you. We wanted Ali Baba."

"He did tell me," I spat back, adding firmly, "And you're not going to get him from me." One of his eyebrows arched in surprise as he studied me, and I thought I saw his lips twitch. Damn it all, he was laughing at me.

"But he's a crook, you hate crooks, you said so yourself."

I didn't like the way he was throwing my words back at me. While I still didn't approve of what Alex had done, I knew there were mitigating circumstances.

"Who says he's a crook? The countess probably gave him the ice just to hook him." I scowled when he smiled at my assertion.

"Need I remind you that it's your employer you're talking about," he cautioned.

"No she isn't. I quit." I took the necklace off and laid it on his desk realizing why he looked familiar. He had Alex's smile. It was a crazy thought and it made me go still as I stared at him.

"This might change your mind," he said, sliding a check across the desk toward me.

I looked down at the check seeing the nice round numbers and cringed. There was no way in hell I'd accept it, I wasn't even tempted. I stepped back, saying, "No dice, tell your client to keep it, maybe buy herself another trinket."

A footfall behind me made me freeze, and I sucked in a shocked breath breathing in Alex's scent, sandalwood and hot man. It couldn't be. I'd left him handcuffed to the bed. But then I glanced at the lawyer's smiling face and groaned.

Something was going on here that I didn't understand. I turned to see Alex standing in the doorway and all my good intentions started to vaporize. His angry glance swept over me rooting me to the spot.

"She wouldn't take the money, adelphos," the lawyer said.

I squeaked in outrage as I made the connection. Brothers. They were playing a game with *me* as the pawn. "Damned right," I bit out, glaring at Alex, daring him to say a word. The possessive look he pinned me with froze me in my tracks. "I'm not for sale, not even as a paid concubine."

"I know," he said softly.

"Bullshit," I snapped back, my defenses still up. This was probably just another game to him, like his cousins playing up to me last night. I couldn't weaken and fall for his charms.

Alex tensed. "Honor, love, you don't understand."

"And I don't want to," I cut in and froze when I heard the alleged countess' voice.

"Thelma, honey, when my brother gets here will you tell him I need to speak to him immediately?"

"He's already here, Athena, but he's busy," Thelma said softly.

I glared at Alex as he continued to pin me with his resolute gaze. If he expected me to overlook his lies, he was in for a disappointment.

"Hey big brother," Athena said, brushing past Thelma to step up to Alex. "I see you finally made it off the crumby island. Did you remember to bring my necklace?" She cast a curious look over the tableau, her sympathetic gaze lingering on Honor, and then she smiled. "Something tells me my brothers have a lot of explaining to do."

"That's putting it mildly," I said, trying not to crumble.

The phone rang and Michael answered it, then gave Alex an apologetic look. "It's for you, adelphos. The word has spread that you're back."

"Not for long. I'm going back on vacation. Tell my assistant to take the call."

I gazed at Alex's siblings' shocked faces remembering he'd told me that he kept things together. He wasn't a crook, he had an office and probably a nine to five job but he was a liar. Maybe if he was occupied I could slip away without breaking down. I started to slip by him and he glared at me, blocking the door.

"Running out on me again?"

"No. I'm going back to my hotel."

"Don't bother. I took the liberty of checking you out and moving your things here for safekeeping."

131

My jaw dropped when I noticed my suitcases in the corner. "You've taken way too many liberties," I snapped back at him, suppressing the thought that I'd practically begged him to make love to me.

"Back off, big brother," Athena said, touching Alex's arm. "Give her a chance to cool off."

"Fine," he said with a growl, stepping back. "I'll take the call," he said to Michael.

I breathed a little sigh of relief and then Athena walked up to me. "Why don't you follow me to my office, honey. I'm sure you'd like to change."

Tears misted my eyes at her kind words. I didn't think I could change back to the sexually repressed woman I had been, and truthfully, I wouldn't want to.

"Thanks." I grabbed my rolling suitcase and followed her.

We entered her office, and I stood there feeling awkward in my harem costume. When she pointed me toward her private bathroom, I smiled and pulled a change of clothes out of my bag. "I'm sorry if I caused a scene."

"Think nothing of it," she said with a smile. "It happens all the time."

"You mean Alex captures concubines all the time," I said, amazed at the surge of jealousy that swept through me. He wasn't the only one feeling possessive.

"Oh, is that what he did to you?" she said, her eyes twinkling.

"Something like that," I said, not wanting to mention the fool's errand Michael had sent me on.

"So you two were alone," she said.

I burned when her speculative gaze raked over me. "Until last night. Nick and Karim came by."

"Oh no. Did he and the bros do their stupid loyalty test on you?"

"Loyalty test," I parroted back at her stunned.

She sighed. "It's something the dunderheads do to their prospective mates. They think I don't know about it," she said with a shake of her head. "Men, they can be such idiots."

So, that's what his hunky cousins had been up to last night. Did that mean that Alex actually thought of me as more than a fling? I was almost afraid to let myself think about the possibility.

"I thought at least Alex had outgrown that stupid pact. I'm surprised he worked up that much passion.

Between you and me, my big brother is a bit of a stick in the mud."

"He wasn't with Risa," I shot back

"Ah, he told you about her, interesting. He never talks about her."

"She broke his heart," I said, knowing I couldn't compete with a ghost. No wonder he hadn't been honest with me.

"No. It was more like she tore his guts out. He hasn't been serious about a woman since."

It explained why he'd lied to me, kept our love affair from getting personal, at least for him. "I've got to go," I said, picking up my bag. "Is there a back way out of here?"

She studied my face and then nodded, opening a door to the outer hall. "Just remember this, you're the only one he's put to the test."

"What about Risa?" I asked.

She shook her head. "He wouldn't do it."

I stood there frozen, my heart wanting me to stay, my mind yelling at me to run. "I have a plane to catch," I said, backing away. The next step, if there was one, would have to come from Alex.

I was still alone in my studio three lonely months later. Alex hadn't come after me, but he had sent me the photographs we'd taken. It was sweet torture looking at them, but they'd inspired me to create my collection. I knew I'd never get over him, but at least I had the visual reminders of that special time we'd shared.

I'd severed all ties with Hal, and quit my part time jobs in order to devote more time to getting my show ready. Once my friend Sherri had started displaying my work it'd literally flown off the shelves, shocking both of us and giving me a big boost to my ego, keeping me going. And the paintings I'd done from my stay on the island were among my best. I knew I had Alex to thank for that. At least he'd left me with something.

A knock on the door made me put down my brush. I walked to the door to find the mailman on my step. I signed for the registered letter and went back inside gazing at the expensive linen envelope. Whoever had sent it, had spared no expense. Alex. My heart leapt but then I looked at the return address and sighed when I saw it said Crown Jewels. Weird. I carefully tore it open and gasped when I pulled out a glossy brochure.

On the cover was the pearl and ruby pendant I'd shown Alex; below it was the title Honor's Heart. My heart skipped a beat. Alex! He had to be responsible for this. The envelope also contained an invitation to the opening and a first class plane ticket to Athens. Could I really risk my heart again?

Chapter Sixteen

Alex all but groaned when Honor walked into the ballroom where the Crown Jewels Spring Gala was being held. Standing silently in the back of the room, his starved gaze took her beauty in. The past three months had been pure torture and it'd taken all his restraint not to go after her.

He'd wanted to kill Athena at first for letting her go, but he'd soon realized that his sister was right. He needed to give Honor her space, let her come back to him when the time was right. She was wearing a little black dress that made the most of her sexy curves. To him she outshone every other woman in the room. She scanned the room, hopefully looking for him, and then walked up to her necklace.

"She's here," he said as Michael walked up to him, with Karim and Nick close behind. All three wearing hand-tailored tuxedos turned to fix Honor with determined gazes. They'd back him up.

"You ready to pull this off," Michael asked.

Alex nodded, taking a deep breath. He'd planned this moment with military precision; it had to go off without a hitch. "Once I take her into the suite your job is to see that we're not disturbed."

When all nodded he turned to glance back at Honor. She was attracting way too much male attention as several men in the crowd gave her the eye. He started toward her, his resolute stride making several of the men turn away.

Damned right, she was his. She turned as he approached her as if she felt his gaze on her and he sucked in his breath, dazzled.

"Hello, Honor," he said, closing in on her. Her eyes widened with sensual awareness and her lips parted but she didn't move away. He took it as an advantage.

"I wondered if you'd be here." She smiled up at him.

Alex stifled a groan as her perfume wrapped around him taking him right back to the last night he'd spent in her arms. "Yet you came anyway."

"Don't read too much into it, Alex." Her teasing gaze flicked over to the pearl and ruby necklace. "There is the little matter of my necklace."

He nodded. "I do owe you for that."

"No, Crown Jewels does," she said with a grin.

"It's one and the same, but I think you've already figured that out."

"I have," she admitted and blushed. "I googled you after you sent me the plane ticket, Sheik Alexander Kahn. Are you really a sheik?" she asked, intrigued.

"I am," he said. "Is that a problem?"

She shook her head. "Not from my point of view. Then you're willing to compensate me?"

"Maybe I'll let you take it out in trade," he said, enjoying her blush.

"An interesting proposal," she said, smiling.

"Come with me. I've got something to show you." He felt her delicate shudder as he took her arm and it reverberated right through him. His cock ached for her and he knew there was no way he could let her go. He walked her into the next room and flicked on the lights, enjoying her gasp when she caught sight of her paintings on display.

"You're the one..."

"Buying your paintings. Yes. I needed leverage."

She turned to smile at him. "Leverage. What are you up to?"

"I hoped the invitation would work. If that didn't work, I was going to lure you with a showing of your art."

Honor giggled as Michael, Nick, Karim, and Athena filled the doorway behind her preventing her from running away. "Now why do I feel ganged up on?"

"Maybe because you are," Alex said, pulling her into his arms. "Love, the only one you need to worry about is me."

Athena cleared her throat. "What my brother is trying to say is that he loves you."

Alex grinned as his family closed the door, ensuring their privacy. "My sister is right. I love you."

I moaned as my sheik carried me toward a thick Persian carpet. His touch was like a brushfire setting off heat throughout me. When he lay me down and bent to kiss me, I held out my arms in an open invitation. "I love you too, Alex."

His eyes glittered as he came down on top of me, one of his big hands cupping my breast, his other hand caressing my ass. I trembled as a moan poured from my mouth. "I need you now."

"Not half as much as I need you," he said, unzipping my dress.

I smiled when he pulled it off me and gazed hungrily at me in my black lace bra and thong.

"God I've missed you, Honor," he said in a low tone. "Promise you'll never leave me again."

"I promise," I said, burning as his sexy whiskey brown eyes ran over me. "I wouldn't find the strength to run from you again."

"Hell, honey. I'll never give you another reason to go," he vowed.

I gave him a smile as he quickly stripped off my bra and thong, noting that his hands were trembling just a little. Lying on the thick Persian carpet naked, above they are on the couch-I blushed as his heated gaze swept over me. I'd probably never get over being shy when he admired me. It reminded me the first time he'd set eyes on me. "Happy birthday," I said, opening my legs for him.

"Alexander, Sheik Alexander Kahn," he said with a smile, his hand slipping down my body to cup my mound.

"As in being carried off into the burning desert by my sheik?" I teased, gasping when he rubbed my clit with his fingertip.

He smiled, doing it again. "It can be arranged."

"Good," I said, dazzled as he played with me, knowing there was nowhere else I'd rather be.

The End

Honey loves writing erotica and hopes that her stories add a little spice to her reader's lives.

Honey Jans lives in a small Midwestern town with her husband and true inspiration. She is a born romantic with an extraordinarily vivid yet kinky imagination.

In February 2005, Honey was overjoyed when "The Gift" became a #1 best seller at Whiskey Creek Press. Then in July, the list went up and "April Love" was at the top, "The Commander's Club" climbed the charts and hit #1 in September, and again in December, Honey was positively delighted. "The Gift" was also a finalist in the 2006 EPPIE Awards Contest and she couldn't be happier.

In her spare time, Honey enjoys lounging under a shade tree and sipping a cool drink while reading a good book. Her talents and interest are not limited to Romance,

Erotica or printed words. Honey is also an artist, with an amazing talent that she inherited from her mother. She lives life to the fullest traveling whenever she can, frequently taking tropical vacations and Caribbean cruises with her husband.

Honey hopes her erotic tales add spice and reading pleasure to your life. She loves to hear from her readers and tries to answer all quires. If you'd like to contact her, you can eMail Honey or join her newsgroup. She is a member of Romance Writers of America, WisRWA, Outreach, Passionate Inc. and EPIC.

More stories from Honey Jans

Whiskey Creek Press Torrid

Candy Kisses
A Torrid Celebration!
Dangerous Liaisons: Bound To Serve
Cindy Revisited
Dare To Be Wilder Honey
Monica's Manhunt

A Wolf's Tale

Double Fantasy

The Commander's Club

April Love

The Gift

Dangerous Liaisons: Stealing Secrets- Coming Soon

Dangerous Liaisons: Enemy Mine- Coming Soon

Once In Love With Laura- Coming Soon

Loose Id

Blue Moon Magic: Twice In A Blue Moon